GRETTA MUL

Araby

Flamingo
An Imprint of HarperCollins*Publishers*

Flamingo
An Imprint of HarperCollins*Publishers*
77–85 Fulham Palace Road,
Hammersmith, London W6 8JB

Published by Flamingo 1998
1 3 5 7 9 8 6 4 2

Copyright © Gretta Mulrooney 1998

Gretta Mulrooney asserts the moral right to
be identified as the author of this work

The poem 'On the Death of His Wife' by Muireadach O'Dalaigh,
translated by Frank O'Connor is reprinted by permission of the
Peters, Fraser and Dunlop Group Limited on behalf of the Estate
of Frank O'Connor

Photograph of Gretta Mulrooney by Niall McDiarmid

The characters and events in this book are fictitious. Any similarity to real
persons, living or dead, is coincidental and not intended by the author.

A catalogue record for this book
is available from the British Library

ISBN 0 00 225688 6

Set in Galliard by
Rowland Phototypesetting Ltd, Bury St Edmunds, Suffolk

Printed and bound in Great Britain by
Caledonian International Book Manufacturing Ltd, Glasgow

All rights reserved. No part of this publication may be
reproduced, stored in a retrieval system, or transmitted,
in any form or by any means, electronic, mechanical,
photocopying, recording or otherwise, without the prior
permission of the publishers.

ACKNOWLEDGEMENTS

With thanks to East Midlands Arts, who offered encouragement and financial support at the start of my writing career.

A special thank you to my agent, David O'Leary, whose friendship, humour and savvy have been magical.

To Peg and her grandson, Darragh
and for Kath, Hugh, Jim and Mary; my very own diaspora.

ONE

My plane was late taking off because a hijacked aircraft had been diverted to the airport. The captain of our flight chatted to us about it over the intercom and pointed it out as we finally taxied to our runway. It was the yellow-tailed one, he said, adding that he hoped the poor panic-stricken souls on board wouldn't have too much longer in there. We were informed that there would be a tail wind so our flight time to Cork would be just fifty minutes.

I had been panic-stricken myself when I'd turned on the early news and heard that Stansted happened to be the airport designated to receive hijacked planes for London. The report had said that the place was closed off but in the end I'd had no trouble getting there despite the busy late-summer roads, driving in through the TV cameras and tight groups of uni-formed men with guns on their hips.

I was glad now that I hadn't rung my father, alarming him with fears of a long delay. I thought of how thrilled he and my mother would be that I'd actually seen the hostage jet with its canary yellow markings. They had always relished random misfortune, a good disaster; a motorway pile-up, a plane crash, a sinking ferry. Pulling their chairs around the television they would tut and invoke the blessings of God on the poor victims of chance, crossing themselves when a body-bag appeared. Extra interest would be provided for my father if there was any suggestion of sabotage or treachery. Then he would follow the story for weeks, poring over newspapers and cursing the bifocals he had never mastered. The grassy knoll in Dallas had provided him with years of satisfying theory and counter theory; sometimes he would favour the CIA conspiracy then after reading another book he'd switch to KGB and/or Cubans as the assassins of JFK. My mother's attention span was shorter; such reports confirmed her view that life was a series of catastrophes waiting to pounce and so she would mark time until the next, uninterested in fine details. After a solemn prayer for the dead and wounded, uttered in a devout voice while fingering her St Christopher medal, she was ready to turn to a quiz show.

It seemed to me that St Christopher was a disappointment as a patron saint. Travellers who were supposedly under his protection regularly met death and injury. Unlike St Anthony, who in my experience always helped to find lost articles, he wasn't up to the job. Either he'd been given an appointment beyond his reach or he was a slacker. I once mentioned this facetiously during my late teens, when I was home from university. I used to enjoy baiting my mother and seeing her colour rise. I had secretly abandoned the stranglehold of Catholicism by then and thought myself a bit of a sophisticate. I viewed my mother's fervent, superstitious belief with distaste bordering on loathing.

There had been a horrific train crash near Bombay. My mother had been expressing pious sentiments about the lost souls over steak and chips. I felt the food sticking in my throat and wanted to be cruel in the way that young people do who see their parents as stuffy obstacles to progress. I commented coolly on St Christopher's apparent shortcomings, suggesting that maybe they could do with a good management consultant in Heaven, someone who would look at personal specifications and psychological profiles. It must be hard being stuck with a job for eternity; you'd get stale, bored, itchy to try something else. Maybe there should be a big shake-up, with roles reorganized; St Christopher might have a talent for music while St

2

Cecilia could prove skilful at protecting travellers. My mother, unsure of my point but understanding the intended mockery, returned her usual riposte; it was a lot of good my *ejicayshun* had done me if it had turned me into a jeering Judas. She didn't know now why they'd ever sent me to the Jesuits because all they'd done was made me smart. She'd waved a chip at me before dipping it into ketchup. 'Smartness won't cut the mustard with St Peter,' she'd stated, satisfied that I'd get my comeuppance at a later date.

As we were lifted into the air I saw a jeep crawl towards the hijacked plane and I could hear myself describing the scene to my parents, beefing it up; the waiting ambulances and fire engines, a glimpse of a famous reporter who was always sent to disasters standing by the verge and smoothing her hair back between takes. They referred to all the major reporters as if they were old friends. 'There's Bill,' my father would say, swishing the teapot and pointing the spout at the screen. 'Hasn't he put on a bit of weight?' my mother would comment, adding that he'd been in Paris last week, probably living it up at the Moolan Rooge and the Folly Berger. 'Ye'd better watch the waistline,' she'd admonish Bill, wagging her finger at him.

Tiny cups of coffee and bite-sized biscuits were delivered by a stewardess. I sipped and crunched at this miniature doll's house fare, listening to the two women in front of me.

'Of course Ireland's the place to be right now,' the blonde was saying.

'Is that so?' Her brown-haired companion's scalp was showing through thin hair.

'Oh yes; very much a thriving scene. Films being made, celebrities buying homes; Mick Jagger, Liz Hurley. I think Madonna showed an interest. There's been lots of articles in the English papers about the quality of life and lack of pollution.'

'Not a second-rate land of bogs and mists any more then.'

'Oh, not at all. The economy's growing. Youngsters who

emigrated are returning. Even the North isn't putting people off now. And of course there are generous payments to the old, you're getting retired English people crossing the water.'

I nodded my agreement. That had been one of the lures that had drawn my parents back to the homeland they'd emigrated from after the war. Letters from my father's brother crowing about free telephones, fuel and subsidized electricity had been dissected and wondered over. Sums were done and a decision was made, when my father turned sixty-five, to return to 'God's own country'. They had sold their modest terraced house in Tottenham for an eighties-inflated profit beyond their dreams, bought a cottage twenty miles from Cork and banked the difference.

I'd visited as often as I could during the ten years they'd lived there, every spring and autumn and usually at Christmas. They wrote regularly; that is my mother wrote and my father added a line or two at the bottom. My mother's writing was large, her As formed in Celtic style. Her letters were a challenging stream of consciousness because of her scatter-gun punctuation. She strewed full stops with abandon, confusing the meaning; a question mark or even several question marks lined up together were likely to appear in the middle of a sentence where there was no enquiry and odd thoughts were scribbled in the margins, such as 'price of butter gone mad altogether' or 'didn't Mother Teresa look terrible sick last week'. My father's cramped hand always said the same thing; 'Your mother's given you the full works. Hope all is well as it is with us here, T.G.'

The letters spoke of a woman who missed the bustle of London, a woman who'd forgotten that rural silences can freeze you as effectively as any ice. She complained about the price of food, the scarcity of good-quality vegetables, the rain, the lack of a Sainsburys in Fermoy, the battle against the damp along the back wall of the kitchen, the ratty dog from the farm up the road who terrorized their rabbits. There was always a long section dwelling on her major preoccupation, her health;

sciatica, rheumatism, water retention, nervous headaches, hot and cold tingles, acid stomach, palpitations and sluggish bowels were listed with the types of agonies they caused. Pain was stabbing, rippling, smarting, shooting, twingeing, griping or throbbing. An exhaustive list of the most recent medicines she had been prescribed was given, with queries about the side effects of the little yellow tablets or the black and red capsules; could they be causing the dizziness or the morning nausea? I could never make my mother understand that as a physiotherapist, I did not have a doctor's medical knowledge. She knew that I had been to university and sometimes wore a white coat; therefore I should be clued up. The last part of the letter would feed me news of my brother in Hong Kong and I assumed that they did the same to him about me. He and I exchanged birthday and Christmas cards.

And then, just four days ago, an envelope arrived addressed in my father's hand. I picked it up, knowing that something must be wrong for long-standing routine to be broken. My mother had had a touch of women's trouble, the brief note inside said, and she was in the hospital for a couple of days while they did tests. *Women's trouble*; what on earth could he mean? My mother was well past the page where that euphemism was usually applied, alluding to gynaecological problems.

I rang him, always a difficult manoeuvre as he was partially deaf, and he sounded relieved to hear me. Too relieved, I thought, a small bell of alarm sounding. I'd get a locum in and fly over, I told him and he shouted back yes, yes, he understood and I had to hold the phone away so that his thin old man's voice fussed around the kitchen.

5

The Safety Pin Crossing

I wasn't frightened of flying but neither did I enjoy it. Not once in the ten years since my parents had moved back to Ireland had I taken the ferry, even though I loved the sea, the humming of the ship and the train journey that would have rattled me there through the Midlands and along grimy Welsh valleys to Swansea.

Ferry crossings were laden with the history of journeys with my mother, a fretful brew of memories. Those trips across the unpredictable Irish Sea stood out in my childhood as a particular purgatory. We had made one each summer for fifteen years, visiting my grandmother for a month. My brother had been there for some but being twelve years older than me, he had soon vanished away to Canberra and then Hong Kong, leaving me to travel alone with my mother. My father would join us for the last ten days and come back with us, allowing someone else to deliver the Royal Mail in south Tottenham.

Perhaps my mother simply hated travelling. Any journey that took her beyond the usual confines of her shopping expeditions brought a fixed, recalcitrant look to her face. Certainly, the build-up in the days before we set off to Cork indicated huge anxiety. As a child, I experienced it as part of the ill-tempered fussing that accompanied any major departure from routine and I dreaded it. Bags would be packed and unpacked, tickets double-checked, masses of food prepared. There was always cold roast chicken wrapped in greaseproof paper and if the journey coincided with a dieting phase, plastic boxes filled with grated carrot and shredded lettuce. All of my mother's movements became razor-sharp. She slammed doors, trod fast and heavily through rooms and became accident prone, nicking fingers and bruising herself.

Inevitably, a zip or buckle on a bag would break an hour before departure, causing mayhem. My mother would seize and roughly apply brown tape or jab huge stitches with a darning needle, muttering under her breath that somebody – whoever had used it last – must have over-stuffed it, causing it at last to give way. These things were always another person's fault and it was always her bad luck to be the one who was there when the trap was sprung. As usual, she was the patsy getting the pay-off. While she cursed, the flabby spare flesh on her upper arms wobbling, I would slink away and sit watching the red buses trundle past the window, a sick fluttering in my stomach. I felt hopeless and useless, thinking that there was something I should be doing but knowing that if I tried to help it would go wrong. Then, just as we were about to leave, she would glance at me and find that I was wearing a jacket that made me look like I was on an outing from the orphanage or my hair resembled a duck's ass or the colour of my shirt suggested that I was going to a funeral. Then I would tell myself that I hated her, that never again would I go anywhere with her, that I deserved a mother who wasn't grossly fat and bad-tempered.

When I was ten years old there was the journey that I called The Safety Pin Crossing. The sea boiled around the boat. It was crowded with high-season travellers. We couldn't afford berths and we struggled through the swaying bodies, hampered by carrier bags, trying to find seats for the night. I've since heard the ferries to Ireland referred to as cattle ships and it was an accurate description then; the passengers were tightly packed, anxious, breathing each other's fetid air, fighting their way to taps for water or to toilet bowls to be sick.

We found one empty seat near the end of a row. On the adjacent seat sat a bulging rucksack, ownership firmly declared. My mother bowled it carelessly onto the floor of the aisle and shoved me down, plonking herself beside me.

'Jesus, Mary and Joseph,' she said, 'I'm destroyed. Me feet are like burst spuds.'

She rustled the food bag and extracted a lump of chicken, tearing the goose-flesh skin off with her nails. I refused food, anxiously waiting for the rucksack owner to appear. The ship ploughed and rolled out of the harbour and the sight of glistening chicken flesh made me nauseous. The owner of the displaced bag was young and tall and he turned up after five minutes with a can of beer. He looked at me and gestured with the can.

'Could the young fella move, Mrs?' he said to my mother. 'That's my seat.'

My mother offered him a blank gaze. 'Pardon?' she said in the mock-English accent she employed when she was on her dignity. It was modelled on the Queen Mother's refined tones, although my mother always referred to her as Lady Elizabeth Bowes-Lyon, as if they'd been on nodding terms in their youth.

'That's my seat,' he repeated. 'I left my bag on it.'

She looked around, mystified. 'We found it empty.'

He retrieved his rucksack from the aisle and balanced it between his legs, pointing at it. 'I left this on the seat. Someone must have moved it.'

She rubbed her chin with a greasy finger, blinking. 'I don't know about that. These seats are ours.'

I stared at the floor. In these situations I repeated my seven times table over and over inside my head until it was safe to breathe again.

'You're winding me up,' he said. 'There's nowhere left to sit now.'

'I'm sorry for yeer trouble but what can I do? Me son's diabetic, he can't stand for long. Are ye all right, pet?'

She gave my arm a gentle push and I nodded, my cheeks healthily fiery.

'Seven sevens are forty-nine,' I ranted to myself, focusing on his desert boots.

8

'It's not fair,' he said, but you could tell that he was backing off. They usually did.

'Ye'd hardly ask a diabetic child to stand while a fine strong fella like yeerself lolls in a chair,' my mother said loudly.

Defeated, he picked up his rucksack and stomped away.

'Would ye look at the cut of him,' my mother said to the woman next to her. 'He looks as if he was dragged through a ditch backwards. Would ye like a chicken leg?'

A small triumph accomplished, my mother puffed up and moved into social mode. Conversation ensued with the swapping of family details. She was all graciousness, sympathizing about her companion's bereavement and promising a novena. The reek of vomit pervaded the decks and people staggered by, mouths covered with handkerchiefs. After a while I rested my head against my mother's cushiony arm, my nose on the indented circle left by vaccination. The slippery material of her Tricel dress shifted scratchily beneath my cheek, its polka-dot pattern dancing under my eyelids as they drooped. There was a familiar smell of warm sweat perfumed by the face powder she applied for public appearances, imparting an odd orange glow to her skin. At other times I might have been pushed off because she was too hot or my forehead was too bony but now she was in good humour and replete with chicken. So I dozed, hearing my mother's voice in the distance; '. . . me son, Dermot . . . off to a good position in Hong Kong . . . ye can't beat a bank for security . . . oh this one here, Rory . . . I had terrible trouble . . . these hot flushes are pure murder . . . aren't nerves the devil incarnate . . .'

I woke just after midnight to find that my mother had a splintering headache and we had to go and find if they had any Aspirin at the First Aid station. The chicken was fighting a rearguard action in her stomach. Everyone around us was asleep, heads dangling. Snores lifted and dipped with the ship. We rambled like drunks to the deck above, following the arrows to First Aid. My mother slapped the bell on the counter and after a minute a stout woman dressed in a nursing outfit

9

appeared. She was as fat as my mother and her uniform was tight, trussed around the middle with a wide belt. She had various badges marching across her chest, attached with safety pins.

'Yes?' she said in a Welsh accent, her chin jutting.

My heart sank. I knew that this woman would be more than a match for my mother who wasn't keen on the Welsh. She thought them squat and shifty. A Cardiff man had once overcharged her for a pound of bacon in Cooper's on the High Street.

'I've a terrible head,' she said in a whisper. 'Have ye any Aspirin?'

'I don't dispense Aspirin,' the nurse said in a clear ringing voice. 'Passengers can't expect that kind of thing. I'm here for emergencies.'

'Just a couple would do,' my mother pleaded, holding her right temple. 'I've a darting pain just here. It's me time of life . . .'

'Can't do, Aspirin's the sort of thing you should bring with you,' the nurse said combatively.

'Ah now, surely it's not too much to ask,' my mother challenged, her tone stronger. She pushed her glasses up her nose, a sure sign that she was ready for a fight.

'Company policy, see,' the nurse stated with satisfaction. 'Emergencies only.'

'So if I cut me wrists ye'd give me an Aspirin?' my mother demanded.

The nurse looked disapproving. 'I'd get your head down if I was you,' she said, dismissing us and moving back towards her office.

'I wouldn't expect much from an ould jade like you,' my mother snapped. 'An ould jade held together with safety pins. Ye and yeer ould boat – safety pins is all that's keeping you afloat.'

The nurse slammed her door and my mother gave the desk bell a farewell ringing slap. Honour satisfied, we rolled back to our seats. I was thankful that the ship was asleep and there had been no witnesses. My mother cooled her temples with 4711 cologne and we broke into the grated carrots. They tasted fresh and sweet in the sour-sick air of the cabin. Midnight feasts were the best ones, my mother said, digging me in the ribs and chuckling. She downed a fizzing bottle of soda water and, burping loudly, said that that felt better, it must have been the wind giving her gyp. She crossed her ankles and waggled a foot, saying that we'd the back of the journey broken now. Her right arm around me, she clasped my head into her huge swell of bosom.

'Settle down there now, dotey,' she said, 'and we'll be in Cork before ye can blink.'

TWO

I hired a car at Cork airport, my usual practice. My parents would shake their heads, saying that I shouldn't waste my money when my father could pick me up. But I knew that the arthritis riddling his bones made driving for any length of time an endurance test. Also, I needed to know that I could get away sometimes during my stays, especially on days when my mother was sunk in gloom, dwelling on her real or imaginary pains.

Ever since I could remember, she had been a mass of symptoms. I had no idea what she actually suffered with and what was conjured up. I supposed it didn't much matter; to her it was all real. The National Health Service had always been her Aladdin's cave, a box of goodies for plundering. She had been so impressed at its inception after the war, she seemed to think she had a life-long duty to make full use of its services. Compared to health care in Ireland where you still had to pay for the doctor's visit, it represented all that was best about England, especially in the fifties, a decade awash with free vitamins and orange juice. The remedies she was given were put on trial when she got them home; if they didn't bring dramatic relief within a couple of days they were discarded with allegations that they were causing heart irregularities or looseness of the bowel. If the medication was ineffective but she liked the look of it she would arbitrarily double the dosage; for my mother, more always meant better. When she met church buddies in the street she would chant her dosages like a litany, going over with relish the numbers and orders of medicines she had been told to take. 'Under the doctor' was one of her favourite phrases, imparted with a significant nod. Visiting the surgery gave her days a shape and meaning and staved off boredom. Tending to her health was a career and each new symptom and medication a promotion.

Her illnesses framed my childhood, trapping and bewildering me. She had taught me to count using her bottles of pills. I had picked the shiny orange and black capsules from her palm, lining them up on the table in tens. We'd done adding up with the round yellow tablets and the oval-shaped pink ones and multiplication with bright red bullet-shaped pills. In primary school, when we sat chanting our tables, I would see those red pills, the colour of phone boxes, dancing before my eyes. Whenever the teacher introduced sums involving questions of the sharing out of sweets or money, I pictured the ranked lines of tablets on the shelf over the radio or thought of Mr Hillard the chemist, who blanched when he saw my mother steaming towards him with yet another prescription.

Whether the washing had been done, the dinner cooked, the shopping fetched or the fire lit, depended on the state of her constitution on any particular day. Everything was unpredictable and subject to change at the last minute; a morning that had started promisingly would degenerate because a headache/attack of nerves/shooting pain in the stomach/hot sweats dripping down her skin or swelling of the legs had suddenly disabled her. I used to look at school friends and wonder how their mothers managed to stay healthy. There seemed to be some obscure code I hadn't broken. I would envy them, knowing that they wouldn't reach home to find a groaning figure splayed in a chair amidst the detritus of the breakfast dishes; they wouldn't immediately be asked for a cup of weak luke-warm Bovril and two of the blood pressure tablets by a frail voice emanating from behind a pair of home-made eye shades.

13

The thought of her on bad days used to make my teeth ache. Her dramatic maunderings struck me into a paralysed silence; what could be said to someone who found no solace in words? As I got older that silence was tight with rage and I would ignore her and her requests for drinks and tablets, telling her to take a walk outside and think about something else. But now, as I stepped on the accelerator, I was acknowledging that you weren't usually admitted to hospital for imaginary pain.

The drive from Cork took forty-five minutes. I rolled down the window and inhaled deeply. The air was peat-smoked and fragrant. My parents' cottage was on the outskirts of a small village, looking down into the valley. I stopped the car momentarily on the curve of the road to examine its whitewashed walls and glossy blue windows. Smoke idled from the chimney. It was just like one of the houses pictured on the sleeves of the terrible records my mother used to play in London. 'If We Only Had Old Ireland Over Here' was her favourite. It featured maudlin songs about cruel landlords, grieving silver-haired mothers and lonely travellers far away from Erin's fair shores. They made me hot with embarrassment, especially in summer when my mother played them loudly with the windows wide open. During my teens I would hide upstairs, shamed because they singled our family out as different and because I instinctively loathed the sentimentality of the lyrics. My mother would sing along in her trilling soprano while I was reading up about the swinging London which seemed to be mysteriously inaccessible even though it was happening all around me. I would tune the radio to Sandie Shaw or The Beatles to drown her out. Her favourite singer was Bridie Gallagher who had a rich, swooping voice. I imagined Bridie as a big-busted woman with a perm, the kind you often saw in small Irish towns.

My father came out to greet me, his braces dangling down over his legs and shaving foam on his chin. I hugged him, inhaling his combined smells of rough-cut tobacco and supermarket soap. He patted my arm, embarrassed by the contact.

'The roses are nearly over,' he said. 'Your mother's been on at me to prune them. I bet she mentions it again today.'

'How is she? This seems to have been very sudden.'

'Oh, not so bad. They've done the tests now, just waiting for results. I was hoping you'd talk to the doctors when we go in, you'll understand it better.'

I knew from the way he bent down to examine a rose bush that he didn't want me to ask him any more about what had happened, this event that was specific to women.

'I imagine she hates the hospital food,' I said, to let him off the hook.

He straightened up, back on safe territory. 'Oh! Don't talk to me! She has me worn out fetching in ham and such. And goat's milk it has to be now; she says cow's upsets her.'

We went in. I made tea and prepared cheese with brown bread while he finished shaving. Everything in this small cottage was familiar, especially the trail of disorder that my mother always spread around her. All of their belongings had been transposed from Tottenham and situated, as far as was possible, in the same places and patterns. If I closed my eyes, I could imagine that I heard the throaty hum of a red bus. The only new thing they had bought for the house in ten years was a tea strainer because the ratty dog from the nearby farm had run away with the old one. Over the back of a chair lay a gaudy half-finished blanket with my mother's crochet hook threaded and ready to go – she kept up a steady supply for the African mission she supported. I could only hope that the recipients liked bright, clashing colours. My father had seized the chance to make the kitchen ship-shape in her absence. His book, upturned on the table, was a spy story in large print.

'It's been too quiet without your mother,' he said, coming in. 'I've been missing my orders. Hard-boiled eggs have been requested for today's menu. Can you do my top button for me?'

Since smashing his elbow on an icy pavement in the

15

seventies, he had been unable to flex his right arm fully. The joint was fused together with a metal pin. I could remember him walking the floor with pain during the nights before the operation, treading quietly so that he wouldn't wake us. It had struck me that his genuine illness had to play a bit part while my mother's trumpeted afflictions strutted centre stage. I reached up and fixed the shirt button, smoothing his collar.

She was in a small ward for six. It was named after St Martin de Porres which would please her because she had prayed hard for his canonization, signing a parish petition to the Pope. For some unfathomable reason she was keen that there should be more black saints. I wondered if it was her own brand of political correctness, trying to ensure that Heaven had its quota of coloured representatives among the higher echelons. I had heard her express regret that Nelson Mandela wasn't a Catholic as he presented good potential for sainthood, with just a matter of a few miracles to be discovered. Her second favourite holy man was St John Macias who had an olive-tinted skin and was known as the soft-hearted saint because he couldn't bear to see suffering. He had once intervened with God to effect the rescue of a drowning sheep and was said to have wept blood when he came across a starving old woman. My mother had copied a line from one of his prayers into her mass book; 'The world is hard and life can be cold and pitiless.'

I could see her as we opened the door of the ward, sitting on her neatly-made bed, her towelling dressing-gown buttoned up and her hair brushed back. She looked like a resentful child who's been dressed to go out and warned not to get mucky. She waved when she saw us and beckoned us on.

'I told yeer father not to go bothering ye,' she said, 'but he never listens to a word I say.' She leaned closer, lowering her voice. 'Pull the curtains round. The ould one in the next bed wants to know everything, she has pointy ears from eavesdropping.'

I arranged the curtains as she wanted them, pulled to overlap so that no one could see us. From habit, I cast an apologetic glance at the woman a few feet away, just in case she'd heard the aspersions on her character but she was absorbed in a magazine and a huge pack of wine gums.

'Have ye brought grub?' my mother asked.

'I've got it.' I took out the pack containing cold chicken, eggs, ham and plain yogurt.

'Ham,' she said, 'I hope they didn't palm any old fatty bits on to ye.'

'It's the best cut,' my father protested, 'off the bone. I watched it being sliced.'

She examined it and nodded. Then she despatched my father for orange juice, giving strict instructions not to buy a brand that was full of pulpy bits.

'Well,' she said, when he'd gone, 'what do ye make of this?' She folded her hands across her stomach and made a steeple with her thumbs; her most confiding gesture. It would be all right to talk to me about what had happened because although I was male, I worked with bodies and had studied fat medical books. To my great mortification she had told several members of the Legion of Mary that she'd always known I'd do some kind of healing work; I had cool hands and a gentle manner. When she had hot flushes in her early fifties she would call me and ask me to put my lovely cool hands on her forehead.

'Spill the beans,' I told her. 'What led up to you coming in?'

She glanced around, even though the curtain was a protective shield. It was her constant worry that other people might get to know her business. It never occurred to her that maybe no one was interested.

She'd woken up one morning to find that she'd been bleeding from 'down there', she told me. My father had called the doctor and she'd been admitted to hospital. Some kind of scan had been done and uncomfortable internal things.

'Have you been having other bleeds?' I asked her.

She said no but she looked down at her fingernails. 'I'm

17

having to wear one of them sanitary yokes,' she said ruefully. 'I thought them times were over.'

They ought to be, I thought, worried. She hadn't worn those since the days of belts and thick looped pads that chafed the thighs. Stick-on winged discretion would be unfamiliar territory for her. I had a sense of things being out of kilter.

I knew that unexpected internal bleeding was not a good sign but I wasn't sure what could cause it. I looked at her carefully. She had shrunk a bit more since I'd last seen her, her shoulders sloping further but at seventy-five that was to be expected and she was still plump. Her colour was good, the eggshell brown of summer days in the garden still evident and her skin, the skin that I had inherited, was clear.

'Give me your specs,' I said, noticing her fuggy glasses, 'I'll clean them for you.' They were filthy, as usual, with tiny flecks of potato on the lenses from when she'd last been preparing dinner. Her eyes without them looked crêpey, vulnerable.

'I expect I'll need an operation,' she said fatalistically. 'I should have had one ten years ago of course, but yeer father wanted to move and I couldn't leave him to do it on his own. Now I'm paying the price.'

I sighed quietly. She often referred to this operation she should have had but whenever I'd asked her what it was for she was vague, saying that it was to do with her womb. There was no good reason why she shouldn't have had surgery if she'd needed it – the NHS was still on its feet in London then. I suspected that she was making it up, embellishing something a doctor had once mentioned to her, or that she had ignored medical advice and avoided going into hospital by using my father and the house move as an excuse. It was impossible to make sense of it; the line between imagination and reality where her health was concerned had always been blurred. She had told herself so many stories that even she found it confusing.

My father returned with orange juice which she examined closely before passing approval. It felt awkward with the three of us trapped behind the apricot-coloured curtain. My parents fell silent, oppressed by hospital inertia.

'Did you hear about that hijacked plane?' I asked. 'I saw it at Stansted.'

My mother clapped her hands, energized. 'I saw it on telly last night. Was anyone killed?'

'I don't think so. Some passengers were released early this morning.' I gave them a full account of what I'd seen.

'It's supposed to be refugees that's hijacked it, trying to get away from Saddam Hussein,' my father told us. 'I heard some of them had been tortured.'

My mother crossed herself. Hussein had replaced Khrushchev and Hitler before him as the devil in human form for her. 'Good luck to the poor creatures, may God help them,' she said. 'Don't they deserve a bit of looking after.'

'Ah, they might not get much sympathy in London these days. They might get sent back to that bastard.' My father shook his head.

I left them, saying I needed the loo but intending to find a doctor. At the door I glanced back. My father had taken my mother's hand in his and was showing her pictures of the hijack in the paper. I thought of their response to the story and then of the man in the shuttle bus at Stansted who'd said loudly, to general murmurs of agreement, that the hijackers should be taken away and shot. I was proud of my parents' humanity, their decency, and glad that it ran through my veins.

A nurse showed me to a small cubicle where a young woman was writing up notes. She was introduced to me as Dr O'Kane and shook my hand, saying that my mother had been telling her about me. I could imagine that several extra degrees and doctorates had been added after my name during these discussions and I felt a familiar quiver of anger at my mother's incorrigible urge for verbal embroidery.

'I understand you've been carrying out tests,' I quickly said.

19

The doctor nodded. 'I've got all the results now. We've found nothing.'

'So what do you think the bleeding meant, means?'

'It's hard to know. Your mother has stopped bleeding now. It's not on-going. It could just be a blip, some matter the body needed to eject. We'll keep an eye on her through her GP. She seems well apart from this incident. She's on very strong tranquillizers, though.'

'She has been for years.'

'I see. Do you know why?'

My mother would have said they were for her nerves. I used a more acceptable phrase. 'General anxiety. My mother's always been very concerned about her health. You're not thinking of stopping the tranquillizers, are you?' I'd read that withdrawal for old people was traumatic; as far as I was concerned, my mother was completely hooked and should be allowed to stay that way at the latter end of her life.

Doctor O'Kane shook her head. 'Most doctors wouldn't prescribe such drugs now, of course, they'd look at counselling or other therapies but at your mother's stage in life . . .'

The doctor came back to the ward with me and told my mother that the tests were clear and she could come home the next day.

'You're sure I don't need an operation?' she asked, fiddling with the sheet. Her voice was meek, anxious. She was always on her best behaviour in front of doctors, polite to the point of obsequiousness.

'Quite sure. Just get a bit of rest and stop eating all those lemons, they'll ruin your digestion.' Doctor O'Kane laughed. 'I'm not surprised you've had stomach pains.'

'What lemons?' I asked when she'd gone.

'Your mother's had a bit of a craze on them,' my father explained. 'She has them grated and squeezed and sliced in hot water.'

'I need the sourness. If I don't have that I get this terrible coating on me tongue. What does that jade know about anything, she's just fallen out of the cradle.' Her shoulders had gone back and she was feisty again now that she'd been told nothing serious was happening.

I thought of the morning near my eleventh birthday when she'd kept me off school, convinced that she had heart trouble. Clutching her chest, she made me ring the doctor and ask for a home call. It was in the days before we had a phone and I raced to the phone box, gabbling my message, running back in a fearful sweat to the house, convinced that when I got there she'd be dead. She was propped up in bed saying the sorrowful mysteries of the rosary in a breathless voice. I fretted until the doctor arrived, attempting to clear up so that he wouldn't see the worst of the jumble we lived in. Her bedroom smelled cheesy but she wouldn't have a window open, saying that the row the buses made jangled her nerves. When he marched in I hovered near the bedroom door and listened to him clicking his stethoscope. She weakly explained to him that she'd had severe pains in her chest, just here. I heard him tell her snappily that she should lose weight and stop eating the rhubarb that was causing heartburn. For a moment I froze, thinking that heartburn meant a fatal disease but he continued that her heart was as strong as an ox; being so overweight, however, must put strain on it long-term. Fewer calories and more exercise, he threw at her, pushing past me on his way out and giving me a stern look which seemed to accuse me of complicity in this time-wasting. I hung my head and felt a hot blush on my neck. After he'd gone she'd cast her beads aside, bounded out of bed, cooked a huge fry-up and instructed me not to tell my father about his visit or that I'd missed a day's school. I watched her shovelling down sausages and bacon and swallowed bile, promising myself that she'd never fool me again.

'Ah, but six lemons a day, Kitty, that's going it some,' my father was pointing out.

'Six! Think of all that acid,' I said to her.

She put on her obstinate face, the one I imagined she'd

worn as a toddler when life tried to thwart her. 'They're good for me,' she insisted, 'they clean out me system, keep me from being bunged up.'

I shrugged. There was no talking any sense to her, she'd go her own way, she always had.

The Beardy Fella

It was a hot, sticky summer's day, August 1966. I was fourteen and I thought I looked pretty far out in my cream cotton flares and orange T-shirt from Bazazz Boutique in the High Street. Despite my trendy clothes, I was dissatisfied. I had no money and nowhere to go. I was at that stage of moody adolescence when home seems like a shuttered prison and your parents are an embarrassment.

I could tolerate being seen with my father who was mildly spoken, tall and slim; with his neatly-trimmed moustache and erect bearing he looked vaguely military. The possibility of being publicly associated with my mother made my skin clammy. She was unacceptable from every view point; grossly fat, loud-voiced, horribly gregarious, unpredictable and tooth-less. Pyorrhoea had caused the loss of all her teeth in her mid-forties. She had been supplied with a false set but only wore them for photographs or important occasions, main-taining that they were pure torture. When she did insert these brilliant white gnashers her mouth looked over-crowded and horsey. The rest of the time she gummed her food and spoke indistinctly, spraying spittle. I had started to put carefully planned avoidance tactics into practice. I attended a different mass and found reasons not to help her with the shopping. If anyone called at the house I ducked into my bedroom, shot the little bolt I had fixed to the inside and lurked behind a locked door until they'd gone.

She didn't seem to notice; in fact, during the summer holi-days she sought my company, bored by herself. She had few friends and no job, my brother had emigrated and my father was at work. Most mornings, unless it was a day for a jaunt or a visit to the surgery, she would lie in bed late listening to middle-brow radio and singing along with Doris Day, '*que sera sera*'. At about half-ten she would get up and eat a substantial breakfast; two boiled eggs from one of those double-jointed egg cups, half a loaf of bread smothered with marmalade, a couple of pots of tea and to finish with, a grapefruit to deceive herself that she was following a light diet. She would wash down her happy pills with the dregs of her tea and then install herself by the window, still in her loose cotton nightie, to watch the neighbours and see if she could catch anyone spitting into the hedge.

On that baking August morning I was planning to sidle off to the library where I could sit in the shady reference section and read Frank Yerby whose historical novels were sexually titillating. I was dismayed to hear my mother moving around at half-nine and to find that she was fully dressed in a good Marks and Spencer floral skirt matched with one of her white cotton charity shop blouses. This meant that she was off on a jaunt, probably a bargain hunt.

'Ah, ye're about,' she said, ambushing me as I came downstairs. 'That's great, we'll get a march on the day and we can be back for lunch.'

'What?' I said, mulish.

'I've found a new dealer, a beardy fella. He does house clearances up at Archway. There's a picture he has that I want but I'll need a hand with it.' The gleam of the chase was in her eye.

'I've got plans. I'm going out,' I told her, picking at a flake of peeling paint on the door jamb.

'Where are ye going?'

'The library.'

'Sure ye can go there any time. No wonder ye're short-sighted, with yeer head always stuck in a book.'

'I'm not interested in going to the beardy fella, those places make me feel funny.'

My mother had graduated from second-hand clothes shops

to bric-à-brac emporiums in the mid-sixties; the kinds of places that later on, when old artefacts had become the rage, would call themselves antique centres with names like 'Granny's Attic' and 'Times Past'. In her shopping heyday they were known as 'Fred's' or 'Bert's' and fairly valuable pieces from early in the century went for knock-down prices. She referred to them by the appearance or characteristic of their owners; so the one in Walthamstow was 'The Foxy Fella', the one in Haringey 'Ferrety Nose' and her favourite in Seven Sisters, 'Snakey Tongue'.

I had been dragged around them numerous times, shifting from one leg to another in musty back rooms while she threw herself into the rough and tumble of the market-place. She would beaver around, poking at furniture, peering at pieces of silver, holding china to the light, examining for hallmarks and faults while silent men kept a watchful distance, waiting for her to engage them.

'How much for the tongs?'

'Five pounds to you. They're solid silver.'

'Hmm, I can't see a mark. Are ye sure they're not just silver-plated?'

'Solid silver guaranteed.'

'I'll give ye three pounds ten and that's robbery.'

Because they knew she'd be back again, a cat drawn irresistibly to the cream, they sold. At other times there were no purchases, just the satisfaction of haggling and a point scored.

'That's an outrageous price!'

'Can't go any lower, Mrs, it's not worth my while.'

'Ah well, I'll be off then.'

'See you again.'

'Through the window ye will!'

While all this was going on I would gaze in a trance at stacks of chairs, bureaux, chests of drawers, jugs and candlesticks until the gloom would make me giddy and I'd slip outside and watch her gesturing through the dusty glass.

Despite my boredom I had been thankful for the change of

focus from clothes shops. She still made the odd foray to
the 'nearly new' or charity places; Sue Ryder shops were her
favourite due to a tortuous connection based on the fact that
Sue Ryder was the wife of a war hero, Leonard Cheshire, who
was the friend of Douglas Bader, the pilot who had attempted
to escape from the Nazis despite having tin legs. I think my
mother must have had a crush on Bader or perhaps just on
Kenneth More who played him in the biopic because she spoke
of him in reverent tones and said that she'd rather give her
few pence to a charity that helped the disabled than to them
ould fat cats in the High Street.

Once the thrill of antique hunting took over I was spared
the worst excesses of the second-hand clothes she used to buy
by the bagful. Outings to the nearly-new shops had always
been a rainy day activity, the damp drawing out the must and
lingering residues of sweat from piles of discarded garments.
My mother would scavenge with a practised hand, enthusing
about an alligator belt, a lace collar, a paisley scarf. Yellowed,
misshapen combinations would be held to the light and
stretched to see if they had a breath of life. Candlewick bed-
spreads were examined for signs of moths or a tell-tale trace
of camphor. Unlikely and awful articles were fitted against me;
thick jumpers past their best, the wool lumpy from too many
washes, boys' shorts or trousers with shiny seams and baggy
seats and large outdated jackets that I could grow into. The
base line, the true test of worth, wasn't whether a thing was
attractive and desirable; it didn't matter that it was too big or
lacking buttons, it was *real* angora or lambswool or astrakhan
or pure silk – 'ye could pull that through a thimble' – and it
was bought.

One of my worst memories which can still make me shiver
was the greenish tweed coat with a fur collar that she bought
me one winter. It was three-quarter length, double-breasted,
too big for me and ten years out of date. I twisted and turned
as she did up the walnut buttons and teased out the collar
with a clothes brush. The King of England, she told me,

couldn't wish for a better bit of cloth on his back. It sat on my dejected shoulders like a mouldering blanket, the fur making me sneeze. I knew that I would be a laughing stock if I was seen with it in school so I took it off at the bus stop and shoved it in my bag. For a couple of days I left the house each morning wearing it and shrugged it off around the corner. I froze in the December winds, my teeth chattering in the playground, until I got a chance to nip into the school boiler room and stuff it in the furnace. As the flames licked it I did a little war dance, and worst crime of all, poked my tongue out at my mother as far as it would go. At home I reported sadly that the coat had been stolen from the cloakroom, causing my mother to visit the school and complain. I stood feeling hot in assembly, trying to look suitably bereft, as the headteacher lectured us on the sin of taking from other people and told us how shocked she was because nothing like this had happened in her school before.

I breathed a sigh of relief when the bags full of clothes were intended for my uncle's family in Waterford. He and his wife Una had eight children and my mother despatched a huge brown parcel to them three times a year. I would watch with satisfaction tinged with pity as dresses and shirts which had been the height of fashion circa 1954 were folded into piles for a remote farm where Peter Pan collars and voile petticoats had never been seen. The threat to myself waned as string was tightened and secured with sealing wax and my father commented, apparently without irony, that they'd think all their Christmases had come at once.

My father indulged my mother in the purchases which cluttered up our small house, even when she acquired outlandish items; a walnut commode, an accordion inlaid with mother-of-pearl, a huge Spanish galleon made from matchsticks. When she produced a pair of bagpipes he made a fool of himself trying to press notes from the floppy cloth. I used to wonder if he feared what she might get up to if she abandoned this relatively harmless occupation; he may have been thinking of

27

the time she set about home improvements, knocking bricks from the fireplace and almost undermining the chimney-breast.

On that hot morning she smoothed her Crimplene skirt, head lowered, and fired a crafty salvo.

'I didn't think it was so much to ask,' she said. 'It'll only take a couple of hours at the most. It's just as well I didn't think of meself the time I saved up for the trip to Rome.'

This was a reference to the holiday I'd gone on with the school when I was twelve. My father had said he couldn't afford it but she'd stored up savings stamps, the green ones with Princess Anne's profile on, sticking them in a book until the fare had accumulated. At the time I had appreciated it, but now it felt like an albatross around my neck, as it got a mention whenever she wanted something from me.

I shrugged and pulled a reluctant face. If I didn't go she'd harp on about it for days. 'All right, but it had better not take long.'

She brightened, swivelling her skirt zip to the side of her waist. 'Oh, ye're an angel. Ye won't notice the time flying.'

The sun streamed into the bus as it swept us to Archway. My mother was humming, tucking stray wisps of hair back into the curled up sausage-bun on the back of her neck. I checked my cream flares; it was only the second time I'd worn them and I worried that I might get them smudged. We were on the long seat, opposite a dark continental-looking woman who remarked on the heat. My mother responded that it was fierce warm sure, bad enough to fry your brains. The dark woman removed her cardigan, hot fingers struggling with the buttons, revealing a low-cut bodice and the swelling tops of brown breasts. My mother poked me in the ribs.

'Come on up the bus. I'm not sitting here with that ould one showing all she's got.' Her voice carried in the still air.

The dark woman scowled and turned to stare out of the window behind her. The conductress looked up from her *Daily Mirror* and sniggered, winking at me. She was young and good-looking. I traipsed after my mother, seething. There wasn't much room for me beside her on the two-person seat and I sat scrunched up, my thighs rubbery and a headache starting. I closed my eyes while my mother sang, 'Put another nickel in, in the nickelodeon, all I want is loving you and music, music, music'. A baby grizzled behind us, its cries piercing my skull.

'Wakey-wakey,' my mother said. 'We're nearly there. I could never have slept during the day at yeer age. Ye should take a tonic, something with iron.'

I remembered that years ago I had heard her refer to a great-aunt who had started screaming one market day in Bantry. The nuns had taken her in and kept her until she died. After that day when she threw her groceries into the air and opened her lungs she never again spoke a sensible word. I wondered what had driven her to such a pass.

We trudged up the hill at Archway, my mother bobbing along with little steps and stopping now and again for breath. A bell jangled as we entered the beardy fella's and a man with a luxurious growth of hair on his chin appeared from the dark recesses of the shop, smiling when he saw who it was.

'You're back again then. After the picture, are you?'

'Ah well now, that depends on what ye're asking. I've brought me son – he's a bit of an art conosoor, ye know.'

'Oh,' he said in mock amazement, 'that's too posh for me, you've got me there.'

He lifted a huge frame from behind a bookcase and turned it to the light. I was faced with a tapestry of a solemn-faced Jesus preaching to a multitude. The threads were in violent hues of green and yellow. Jesus had a livid purplish face with murky blemishes resembling chicken-pox scars. His followers were a brown blur.

'You can't buy that,' I hissed, 'it's foul and anyway, we've nowhere to hang it.' As soon as the words left my lips I regretted them, knowing that they would be taken as a challenge.

29

My mother rubbed her fingers along the frame, standing back and looking at it rapturously as if it was a long-lost Van Gogh.

'I think it's gorgeous. Look at the work that's gone into it. There must be hundreds of threads in there and sure somebody did it for the glory of God. How much?'

I moved back and propped myself against a crumbling sofa with horsehair escaping from its seams. A fox's head perched on one of its arms. Dust motes drifted across an ancient wardrobe with age-mottled glass. The air was so dry and thin it was hard to breathe. In Carnaby Street people were swinging and having their hair cut in geometric shapes. I'd read in the *Evening Standard* that Mick Jagger was opening a new boutique there this week. I felt a sullen rage.

The beardy fella was examining the masterpiece. 'Ten quid and that's a bargain. The frame alone is worth that.'

'I'll give ye seven, there's a scratch on the corner.'

'Eight.'

'Ye're a terrible blackguard. All right so.' She was pleased. She took out a hanky and rubbed the glass. 'Will ye give us a hand with it out the door?' she asked him as she passed over notes.

'How are you getting it home?'

'On the bus, me son can help.'

'Blimey! I hope you've got strong muscles, it's bloody heavy.' He cast a doubtful glance at my skinny frame.

'Oh, we'll manage,' my mother said, pushing me ahead of her to the door. The beardy fella manhandled the tapestry after us and left us to it.

'Now,' my mother said chirpily, 'we'll hop on a bus at the corner. Ye go in front.'

The thing was a dead weight and difficult to grasp. We staggered up the road in the blinding sun, panting, stopping every few minutes to massage our fingers. My shoes were rubbing my toes. I felt a pain beginning in my side where the frame was gouging into me. I thought that it must have been like this carrying the cross through Jerusalem; all we needed to complete the picture were centurions and whips.

'Never mind,' my mother gasped encouragingly. 'Not far to the bus now and then we'll be on the pig's back.'

I saw that she'd gone beetroot red and a savage satisfaction gave me the strength to make the last few yards. We leaned the tapestry against a low wall by the bus stop and I sank down beside it. My head was hammering, my mouth dry and sandy. I rubbed my bruised hands and noticed that my trousers were covered in dusty marks. Shreds of horsehair were clinging to the seams.

'See,' my mother said as the bus swayed into view, 'it's only half-eleven. Didn't I say we'd be back for lunch?'

THREE

I spent a few days with my mother after her return from hospital. She seemed hale and hearty. On the first evening back she headed for the roses with the secateurs, saying that they were getting blowsy. I shopped in Fermoy and bought her a packet of sanitary towels, knowing that she'd be too embarrassed to ask for them herself and wouldn't mention such an item to my father. She threw them into the kitchen cupboard, saying that I'd had no need to get them ould yokes, wasn't it all sorted now.

She and my father settled into their routines; feeding and cleaning out the hens, tending the vegetable patch, weeding flowers, collecting juicy nettles for the two rabbits, Collins and Dev. My mother did a good deal of pointing and instructing with her blackthorn stick while my father pulled his old beret down and wielded the hoe. She had started a small herb garden and picked a daily clump of rosemary to put in her pocket. Rolling it through her fingers she sniffed deeply, smiling; it smelled, she said, of Araby.

'Do you still miss London?' I asked her as she watered her busy Lizzies. This was a question I would normally avoid, dreading the tale of loss and loneliness that would pour out. But the frightened look in her eyes when Dr O'Kane approached her hospital bed had touched me and I'd felt protective towards her. I suppose I was trying to reassure myself as much as discover her feelings.

She picked off dead leaves, rolling them in her fingers. 'Some mornings I'd give me right arm to hop on a bus and stop at Rossi's café for egg and chips.'

'You could have egg and chips in Fermoy.'

'It wouldn't be the same. Yeer father would be worrying at me to get home and there's no bus.'

'This is what you always said you wanted when you were in Tottenham; a cottage and half an acre.' For years she'd complained about the traffic and the noise and the smallness of her garden. I remembered her standing at the back door in the summer, looking out on the patch of drying lawn and saying wistfully that it would be a fine day to be in Kinsale.

'So I did, so I did.' Her martyr's voice took over. 'Of course I only came here because yeer father was so keen. He had his heart set on it and I couldn't disappoint him.'

This self-deception left me breathless, even though I'd heard it before. As I recalled, she had been the one to promote the idea; she had bought copies of the Irish papers to look at property. I felt the old familiar guard coming down, the one I'd carefully constructed over the years to protect myself from her manipulations and the webs of illusion that she spun.

' 'Tis terrible lonely here sometimes,' she said.

'You could get to know people if you tried; there's the church.' I heard my tone; even and dry, distancing myself and warning her to back off. This was a record that we'd played many times before and the lyrics were always the same.

'Oh, I can't be doing all that at my age, I'm an old woman.' On cue, she changed the subject. 'Do ye ever see the beardy fella?'

'No.'

'I wonder is he still there. Do you think would he remember me?' She looked across the fields, twirling a flower by its stem.

'I'm sure he would, yes.' I watched her, knowing that she would carry her discontent wherever she went. I thought of those lines from *Much Ado About Nothing*; 'one foot in sea and one on shore'. If she ever reached Heaven there would be a honeymoon period when she would cultivate her preferred saints. Then she would start to find fault with the harps and the constant Glorias, declaring that they were splitting her skull. Saint Peter would be accused of giving her dirty looks.

Back in London I resumed work. At first I phoned each night, then settled back into my usual once weekly call. I was having some tiles replaced on my roof and I watched the workman scale his ladder, thinking that if my mother was here she'd have picked an argument with him before the day was out, alleging that he was hammering too loudly or that he'd scraped the paintwork or knocked over one of her flower-pots. I'd lost count of the number of people she'd fought with, relishing the injection of some drama into her slow-moving days. A plumber who'd come to fix the toilet in Tottenham had been convicted of blasphemy when he'd gestured with his hammer at the picture of the Saviour with the crown of thorns and the moving eyes, asking if it gave us the creeps on dark nights. She had issued many a personal fatwah in her time.

Eight weeks after my return, in the middle of November, I came in one evening and found a message from my father on the answerphone. He shouted slowly, saying that he hoped I would get this but he didn't understand if he'd waited long enough after the signal. He wondered could I come over. My mother wasn't well but she wouldn't let him call the doctor and he was beside himself with worry. Her appetite was gone, he added. He was making this call while she was asleep. She was sleeping a lot, day and night.

I was there the following afternoon. When I walked into the kitchen a sharp blade of shock knifed my chest. She was sitting in the Captain's chair she'd bought from Snakey Tongue, looking into the distance. She had lost a lot of weight from her face and arms but her stomach was bigger than ever. Her hair was greasy and she was wearing an old apron covered in food stains. Her bare feet looked blueish in faded slippers. When I greeted her she looked up at me and focused but her eyes were lifeless. I'd spent enough time around sick people to know that look; in that moment I realized that she was dying. I bent to kiss her and a rank smell wafted upwards.

'Have you not been feeling well?' I drew a chair up.

My father was hovering in the background. 'Will I just feed the hens and make the tea?' he asked.

I nodded when my mother didn't reply. 'You don't look too good,' I said, taking her hand. Her nails were long and dirt-grimed.

'No, I'm not meself at all. I don't think I'm well.' Her voice was low and tired.

'Why won't you see the doctor?'

'Sure he only pokes me about.'

'Yes, but you really should let him check you.'

She tightened her grip on my hand. 'Ye won't put me in a home, will ye?' she whispered.

I felt a momentary impatience that I quelled. There was no pretend drama now, the question shivered with real fear. 'Of course I won't. What makes you think of such a foolish thing?'

'Yeer father can't manage. He won't be able to look after me. Sure he's full of aches and pains himself.'

'Listen, you won't be going into any home. There's no chance of that. All right?' I stroked her hand, feeling the veins under the papery skin.

She nodded meekly and her gaze wandered away again, as if she had lost interest.

'I'm going to ring the doctor,' I told her. 'Have you been bleeding at all?'

She shook her head. 'Just terrible tired. All the grub tastes like ashes.'

My father was throwing grain to the hens. The arthritis in his joints made his movements jerky. He looked as if a strong wind would blow him over.

'She's not good,' he said to me.

'No. Why didn't you tell me sooner?'

'Ah, you know your mother. She has me beat. She wouldn't go to her hospital appointments, then she put a stop on the doctor. He came one day and she wouldn't see him, told me to say she was asleep. I was terrible embarrassed with him driving out from Fermoy and all. She's frightened of going back into hospital. It's because of Nana.' His voice was cracked with fatigue.

My grandmother, her mother, had died in hospital after a stroke. I took a handful of the grain and sprinkled it on the ground. A hen strutted and pecked by my feet. My mother loved her hens, just as her mother had. She would stand at the hen-house door, talking to them, calling them her doteys, clucking to them and asking them to lay her beautiful speck-ledy eggs.

'I've been trying to get her to eat but she won't. She takes a few mouthfuls. I can't wash her properly with the old arthritis, I'm frightened I'll let her fall. I wanted to ring you a couple of weeks ago but she sprang the old tears on me.' He made a gesture of exasperation and scratched his thin, still sandy hair.

He'd never been able to deal with her if she cried. A blank, terrified look would come on his face and he would slope away to his woodwork or his vegetables.

'I've told her I'm calling the doctor. I'll do it now.'

He looked relieved. 'Ah good. She'll take it from you, she knows you've got sense.'

I rang the doctor, a man called Molloy, and caught him just before evening surgery. I'd never met him so I explained who I was.

'My mother is very ill, I'd like you to visit immediately,' I said.

He sounded truculent. 'She's been very naughty, missing appointments. We haven't been able to monitor her.'

I bridled at that word, *naughty*, reducing her to less than adult. What did he know about my mother's fears? 'I realize that she has avoided medics but I'm worried about her. She's lost a lot of weight very suddenly.'

'No cancer was found in the tests,' he said quickly and I

thought he sounded defensive. He would know that I was a physiotherapist, my mother would be sure to have told him, and I guessed that he was wary of another professional.

'No, I know that the original tests were clear. Can you come tonight?'

'Yes, very well. You'll be there?'

I confirmed that I would. I went into my mother to tell her. My father had given her a cup of tea and she was holding it, untasted, in her lap.

'I'm mucky, Rory,' she said. 'Look at me, I haven't even had a cat's lick for a week. What will the doctor think at all?'

I smiled. 'A cat's lick' was the name we'd always given to a quick rub of a flannel on the face.

'Would you like to have a bit of a clean-up?' I asked her. 'I'll wash your hair for you too. You've always liked your hair to look nice.'

I didn't want Molloy turning his nose up at my mother; I wanted her to have dignity as he probed. I wasn't sure how she would react to my suggestion. This was the moment when my mother needed a daughter and I wished for a sister to leave delicate tasks to. I was used to manipulating the limbs and kneading muscles of both sexes, but I had never been in the bathroom at the same time as my mother and the barrier of propriety was a strong one.

' 'Tis a fine state I'm in when me son has to help me wash,' she said but she nodded her agreement.

She let me lead her to the bathroom, walking slowly and giving little groans. Inside she held onto the sink.

'That was my life-blood draining away when I bled,' she said flatly.

I smoothed her hair back, paralysed by this sudden insight. She knew the symptoms of cancer; a woman who lived across the road in Tottenham had died of it and my mother had watched her waste away. She had always said the word in a hushed tone, as if to invoke it might bring its wrath on her. I didn't know what to say. I took the coward's way out.

'You're not well at all, Mum, that's for sure.'

'I should have had that operation, years ago.'

'Maybe. But that's past now.'

'Oh everything's past now.'

There was a silence. My eyes were heavy.

'Shall we do your hair first?' I asked gently, pulling up the chair that they threw towels on.

'I couldn't be climbing on that,' she said fearfully in a child's voice, clutching my arm.

My heart juddered. 'No, no. No climbing. You can sit on this and rest your head back, like at the hairdresser's.'

She acquiesced and I helped her lower herself down. I wetted her hair and poured on shampoo, lightly massaging it in. Her temples had become concave and I imagined that if I pressed too firmly my fingers would penetrate her scalp. Strands of hair came out on my knuckles, threading them together. Her hair had been a source of huge pride, thick and wavy into old age. She would often say that it had drawn many compliments in her youth, a honey-coloured delight. For years she had kept it long because she hated hairdressers. They pulled you about, she said, and made an eejit of you. Her scalp was sensitive and the slightest tug on her hair hurt her; she didn't like anyone touching it. It was still well-coloured with little grey but as I witnessed how thin it had become tears filmed my eyes. This was the first time I had washed my mother's hair and it was slipping away, swirling into the plughole. Her head seemed weightless in my hands and the brown furry ball webbing my nails emphasized that she was giving up, letting her pride and joy go without a fight. Any hope that I had trickled away with the soapy water. I wanted to weep but I reached for a towel, passing it unobtrusively across my eyes before wrapping it carefully around her head.

'Now,' I said, sitting her up as you would a child, 'was that okay? I didn't hurt, did I?'

'No, ye're very good. The water was lovely.'

'I was better than those old jades of hairdressers, then?'

She nodded but I didn't raise a smile. I helped her unbutton her cross-over apron and she stood up so that I could turn the chair around. I soaped a flannel and she ran it around her face and neck and under her arms. The tops of her arms, where there used to be solid quivering fat, were wasted. I turned away and fiddled with the soaps and shaving gear on the shelf behind me, rearranging them. She ran out of energy half way, leaning against the sink rim, so I rinsed the flannel and went back over her skin, wiping away the soap. Her large stomach, slightly exposed beneath the apron, was a yellowy colour. She said that she could manage her other bits herself so I ran fresh water.

'Shall I help you with your knickers?' Although she thought of me as a medic, we'd never been in this kind of personal territory before. I hovered, unsure.

'Just slide them down for me.'

She eased them from the top and I pulled them slowly by their elasticated hems. Then I left her to see if I could find fresh clothes. In the bedroom I searched the chest of drawers and collected clean underwear and a cotton dress. When I got back to her she was resting in the chair, the damp flannel in her hands.

'All done?'

'All done,' she said, 'mission accomplished.'

Putting her clean knickers on was the hardest part of dressing. It hurt her to raise her legs so I had to carefully lift each foot and manoeuvre the voluminous Aertex garment she liked up her calves and thighs. She moved them upwards, leaning against me, her head pressed to my chest.

'Do ye remember the time we were on the bus and ye suddenly told me ye'd no underpants on?' she asked, steadying herself with her arms around my waist.

'Yes. How old was I?'

'Oh, four I think. We were after coming out in a hurry. Ye were always difficult about letting me dress ye, ye'd want to do it yeerself. Ye never wanted to hold me hand in the street.

39

Ye called out about the pants in a loud voice. I was mortified.'

In the kitchen I dried her hair, kicking the clumps that fell to the floor under the seat so that she wouldn't see them.

'Where's yeer father?' she asked, sounding worried.

'He was with the hens and then he was going to get some turf in.'

' 'Tis getting chilly outside, he doesn't want to be catching cold.' She pressed the palms of her hands together. 'I hate it when the evenings draw in, the place is terrible lonely. Call him in, will ye.'

I went to the door and saw that he was opening the gate for the doctor's car.

'Dr Molloy's here,' I told her.

'I can't go to hospital, I've no clean nightdress.'

'That's no reason not to go to hospital. If you're ill, you need to find out what's the matter and Molloy is only a GP. You need the expertise in hospital.' I crossed to her. 'You won't stay in there, you'll come home again.'

'Are ye sure, Rory?'

'I'll bring you home myself.' I kissed her forehead. Now she smelled of peach soap and the talcum she'd asked me to sprinkle over her arms.

Dr Molloy was business-like, which I was grateful for. I was ready to step in if he started taking her to task for misbehaving but when he saw her he just asked her how she was feeling. He spent two minutes examining her, glancing at her stomach, then straightened. He was going to ring for an ambulance, he told her; she must go into hospital that night. She said nothing. My father sat down beside her and said she must try to eat something; how about a bit of an egg custard? The doctor used the phone and I saw him to his car.

'She's dying,' I told him.

He swung his bag onto the passenger seat. 'It doesn't look good. Rapid, whatever it is. I can't say more till the hospital takes a look.'

He accelerated away, his lights fading into the gloom. Once

his car had gone there was silence. The faint barking of the ratty dog from up the road floated on the evening air. I bent down to sniff a late rose that my mother had bought on a trip to the garden centre three years ago. I picked a few twigs of rosemary to put in her pocket, hoping that they would make her think of exotic places in the hospital's antiseptic confines. Turning to the house, I opened the kitchen door. My parents were sitting side by side, hands clasped, looking into the fire.

Nectar

My mother believed in Santa until she was fifteen. When a parlour maid in Youghal laughingly revealed that he was a fiction she cried herself to sleep.

She was born near Bantry, the third of six children. Her father drank and died – I never knew whether from a pickled liver or something else – when she was seven. Her mother struggled to bring her children up on a paltry widow's pension, doing odd jobs locally and bartering eggs for milk and butter. I'd always had the impression that my mother had been frightened of her father; he was an unpredictable, boisterous man from what she said, although she rarely spoke of him. I suspected that he had been a wife beater. My mother placed great value on the fact that my father was teetotal and of a placid temperament.

Food was always scarce when she was a child. The family existed mainly on potatoes and buttermilk. Meat and bought goods were for high-days only. Rations became even scarcer when she took her first job, aged fourteen. She went to work in a grand house near Cork city, for 'a one with a big backside and her creenaun of a husband'. She was a maid of all work: cleaning silver, setting fires, helping the cook, polishing shoes, ironing. Up at six in the morning, she finished at eight in the evening.

When I was a child, I would listen to her often-repeated stories with a sense of *déjà vu*, mildly bored; they had no place in the framework of London and a youth who was desperate to be trendy whilst doing exams and planning to go to university. They sounded like tales from another century, ranking with the reports of boy chimney-sweeps in my history book.

42

Later on when I thought about them I found it hard to imagine what it must have been like for her. She would have missed her mother terribly up in her attic room which she shared with two other girls. A naïve child, she was expected to do the work of a mature woman and cope with the emotional cost of being out in the world alone.

The main theme of that part of her life was hunger. She never got enough to eat. Her rumbling stomach orchestrated the days. Sores developed at the corners of her mouth from vitamin deficiency. Her periods didn't start until she was eighteen because she lacked iron. She would describe the small portions, how the sugar and butter were meagrely allotted and how she would try to slip bits of food into her mouth when the cook wasn't looking, or pinch chunks of carrot or cheese between the kitchen and dining-room. The one with the big backside made marmalade and jam every year. It was kept in a larder at the side of the kitchen. Early in the morning, when the cook was still half-awake, my mother would sidle in there with a spoon and eat from a jar she'd opened and hidden at the back of a shelf. 'Oh,' she would say, smacking her lips at the memory of it, 'that marmalade was pure joy, like nectar.' She could still taste it years later, thick and dark and bittersweet.

One of the dogs had once dashed into the kitchen and made off with a roasted pheasant. The cook chased it but quickly gave up, hampered by her age and girth. My mother continued; she was a slim young thing then and the smell of the pheasant juices on the breeze spurred her on. She cornered the spaniel, grabbed the pheasant from its jaws and gave it a good kick to despatch it. Then she crouched behind a bush with her trophy. She made short work of the meat, tearing it from the carcase and gobbling as fast as she could. Wiping her chin and fingers on her apron, she ran back, waving the skeleton. The dog's name was mud thereafter.

I would think of that story when I saw my mother foraging in the kitchen in Tottenham. An hour after a huge meal she

would be out there, finishing off the apple tart or slicing a cut
of cold meat, the chink-chink of cutlery on china giving her
away. Her appetite seemed insatiable.

When I reached my twenties and dabbled in psychology I
concluded that those early years of deprivation had left her
with a hunger that could never be sated. Before then, when I
was more cruel and callow, she disgusted me. I saw her as a
person with no self-control, no dignity. I was slim and tall,
like my father. As I watched her reach for her sixth potato,
her third portion of stew, I would wonder how I had ever
emerged from that ungainly body.

Meal times were a cavalry charge; my mother had to be at
the table first, loading her plate before anyone else arrived.
She could brook no delay; if there was one, she would start
eating in the kitchen, taking spoonfuls from the saucepans and
continuing to stoke up on her way to the table. She was an
excellent cook, adding touches of refinement that she'd seen
in the big houses she'd worked in. Her pastry was the best
I've ever tasted and she had a way with puddings such as
charlotte russe and chocolate soufflé that she'd served at the
swankiest of gatherings. The spicy fruit cake she threw together
– a fist of this and a fist of that, never weighing but always
achieving exactly the right consistency – was heavenly, especially when warm from the oven. Despite all that I always sensed
the onset of indigestion before I'd lifted my knife and fork.
The table was too laden with emotion; desperation lurked in
the dishes. Once she had satisfied her immediate hunger she
started to press extra helpings onto the rest of us in order to
camouflage her own excess. Refusal provoked the comment
that she didn't know why she bothered, she might as well
serve up TV dinners instead of slaving over a hot stove. I
was only seven when my brother left home, but I dimly
recall him earning praise for his huge appetite; he gamely
tucked away everything he was offered, eating so fast that it
was hard to believe he tasted it. Once he'd gone, my father
and I guiltily ploughed on, trying to accommodate another

spoon of cabbage or slice of sponge cake to humour her.

The dreaded diets brought havoc and much bewailing. Every now and again, when her blood pressure had risen or her hormones were playing up, she trotted to the doctors and returned grim-faced. She tormented every GP at the practice but to no avail; she was always told to lose weight. A diet sheet would be waved, listing terrible menus such as grilled fish, half a potato, a spoon of peas and stewed prunes. Forbidden items were pictured below a skull and crossbones; bread, cakes, casseroles, fried food, pies, all the things she craved. We would shift uneasily, wondering how long it would last this time.

Two weeks was the maximum. She would line up her boxes of calorie-reduced rolls like troops forming for battle. They were large and brittle with the consistency of polystyrene. One of those for breakfast with a poached egg and a glass of hot water with a dash of lemon juice; for lunch a portion of grilled liver with one tomato and a roll; dinner was a piece of steamed fish, the pathetic half potato and a roll and, joy of joys, purée of apricot. We lived the diet with her, shared every groan and imprecation. Guiltily we ate the calorie-blasted dinners she prepared for us, slipping butter onto our plates, going for gravy under cover of the newspaper, palming a sausage while watching sideways as she sliced a roll to reveal that it was made of air pockets. She ate slowly, making the most of every mouthful with the pained expression of an ascetic who has vowed mortification of the flesh. We forced down sugarless apple pies – so that she could scoop fruit from beneath the pastry – our eyes watering and palates tingling. We lied that we didn't want cakes and biscuits, snaffling them quietly while she was in the bathroom or waiting until she'd gone to evening mass or benediction to raid the cupboards.

The anguish of watching her battle became too much at times. I would find myself craving chocolate, ice-cream, sugar-dredged buns, in a way that I never usually needed them. There was one bitterly cold November night that I remember well. I had slipped out to the corner shop after dinner, devastated by the simmered prunes in my pudding bowl. I had to satisfy a desperate desire for a large chocolate bar with mint cream filling. As I reached the counter I saw my father in his belted mac and peak cap selecting a big slab of treacle toffee. We glanced warily at each other, completed our purchases and stepped outside. Wordlessly, we stood by a denuded plane tree and quickly gobbled our goodies, shivering as an icy wind whipped our legs. When we'd finished we returned home in a conspiratorial silence, licking our fingers nostalgically.

'I was out for baccy,' my father hissed at the gate.

'I was getting my magazine,' I confirmed, touching the rolled-up *Look and Learn* in my pocket.

As the diet progressed, my mother's expression would gradually become sourer, her mouth tighter. She drooped and sighed her way to a chair after meals. There was no energy in her legs, she would declare, she was as weak as water; those bleddy doctors were trying to kill her. How could a body survive on morsels? My father would step tentatively into the house at night, asking my brother or me if the diet was still on the go. An affirmative answer brought a deep breath and a scratching of the forehead. He would approach her stealthily, keeping his voice low, ready to beat a retreat.

The day the diet ended was signalled as soon as you entered the house and smelled frying. Crumpled boxes of rolls were rammed into the kitchen bin and the diet sheet lay crisped at the back of the fire. The frying pan sat splendidly charred on the cooker, with traces of sausages, egg, tomato, bacon and mushroom offering evidence of the official cessation. An empty multi-pack of custard fingers stood abandoned on the table, the gaping box speaking of pillage and satisfaction. Tension dissolved through the house and whoever was first back – out of my father, my brother and myself – spread the word of a cease-fire to the other two, grinning with relief as our stomach muscles relaxed.

FOUR

The ambulance men were cheery and kind, wrapping a blanket around my mother and making her snug. They lifted her carefully into a wheelchair to take her out, but the slightest jolt made her wince and I heard a gasp of pain as they manœuvred through the narrow front door. I don't have children, but I've heard friends who are parents say that they would do anything to take their children's pain away, to make things better. I felt that about my mother as her newly-washed hair was skimmed by a breeze coming across the valley. She gripped the arms of the wheelchair and asked if I had remembered to pack her rosary; yes, I said, it was in her bag.

My father travelled with her in the ambulance. I drove behind in my hired car, flinching for her at each dip in the rutted road. I felt a sense of powerlessness, as if she was being kidnapped and I couldn't catch the people who had taken her. Being snatched away had been one of her greatest fears for her children. I had received numerous warnings from a very young age to avoid dark city streets and the approaches of strangers. White Slave Traders had caught her imagination after she'd read an article in the *Sunday Express*, and she had alarmed me with talk of men who enticed children and whisked them away to Eastern countries to be playthings. As she grew older she found life more and more alarming and the possibilities of personal harm endless; being knocked down, crashing in the car, contracting a sudden and deadly disease like bacterial

meningitis, expiring in the dentist's chair. These things were
real, they had happened to other people. In the late seventies
a woman was killed instantly in Harrow when a youth threw
a large parsnip from the window of a moving car, striking her
in the head. My mother was aghast; even vegetables couldn't
be trusted. Often I would turn my key in the door to find it
bolted and she would demand to know who was there through
the letterbox.

At the hospital she was wheeled away to see a doctor. My
father and I waited in a small airless room with copies of
pictures by Impressionists hanging crookedly on the walls. He
massaged his legs. Evening was his worst time for pain and he
looked drawn. He always slept badly, waking every couple of
hours during the night and getting up to brew tea and read.
During the day he cat-napped, making up the lost sleep, but
this routine had been thrown.

'Have you brought your tablets?' I asked him.

'In me pocket. It's another hour before I can take them.
They wear off quicker and quicker, me system gets used to
them.' He shrugged. 'We're a great pair of old crocks, aren't
we?'

'It's all that fast living years ago,' I told him.

'Oh! You're right, we should have kept away from the
fleshpots.'

They'd hardly ever gone out; just the occasional church
whist drive and the cinema now and again, films with a
religious flavour like *The Ten Commandments*. Sunday jaunts
in the car to Epping had been a popular pastime. My mother
liked going into country churches and pointing out loudly
that they would have originally been of the true faith, before
that monster Henry the Eighth got above himself. 'Of course,'
she'd once told a startled vicar while I lurked behind a brass
shield, 'this is stolen, it was one of ours, the only Holy Catholic
and Apostolic Church.'

'Is it all right to have a smoke, do you think?' my father
asked.

48

I looked around. 'I can't see a no-smoking sign.'

He took out his tin and rolled a thin cigarette, pinching off the wisps of stray tobacco and letting them fall to the floor. They reminded me of my mother's hair, drifting down.

'I got her to have a bit of boiled egg anyway, something to line her stomach.' He got up and wandered to the window.

After a short while a nurse came and told us that my mother was going to be transferred to a ward and we could go up with her. She was in her nightdress – the one clean one I'd managed to find – and looking downcast.

'How are you?' my father asked.

'Don't talk to me. They treat you like a slab of meat.'

We rode up in the lift in silence. Two nurses helped her into a bed. One of them turned to me and said that we should only stay a short while because the registrar would want to come and see my mother. The younger of the nurses, a student, pulled a chair up and said that she just needed to ask a few questions. She had a clipboard with a form attached.

'What name do you like to be called by? Is it Katherine?' she asked, pen poised.

'Kitty.'

'Do you have any special dietary needs?'

My mother shook her head.

'Do you have a religious belief?'

'RC,' my mother said.

'How about leisure activities? What do you do for a hobby?'

My mother gave her a look of incomprehension and shivered.

The ward was tropically hot. I wanted to snatch her clipboard and shout, 'Can't you see she's dying, for God's sake! She can't eat and hobbies are the last thing on her mind.' Instead I said that my mother liked TV and asked that the rest of the questions be left for the moment. The nurse looked put out but clasped her clipboard to her chest and moved away. My father fussed around taking my mother's talcum and wash things from her bag and installing them in a locker.

'Ye think I'm going to be here for a while, then.'

'Ah, Kitty,' he said, 'I'm only trying to make things comfortable.'

'Ye'd better let Dermot know I'm in hospital, he'll want to come and see me.'

'I'll ring him,' I told her.

'Me feet are like blocks of ice. Would they ever have an ould hot-water bottle?'

I put my hand beneath the sheet and felt her feet, rough with corns and hard skin. They were freezing. I chafed them with my hands, kneading the toes gently. I was wearing socks and trainers; I unlaced my shoes and took my socks off, then slipped them onto her feet.

'Oh, they're warm,' she said. 'Ye're warm-blooded.'

'I'll ask the nurse for a hot-bot as well,' I said.

She looked small in the high bed. I found the older nurse who'd helped her into it but was told that the hospital didn't have hot-water bottles.

'If I go and buy one, will you fill it?' I asked.

She looked dubious. 'I'm not sure it's allowed, it might burst and scald her.'

'It will hardly burst if it's new. Her feet are cold and she hates being cold. She's frightened, her circulatory system isn't working properly. It would bring her a little bit of comfort.' My voice was rising with impatience.

She looked around. 'Well, I suppose . . .'

'Thanks,' I said. 'I'll pop out. Is there a late-opening chemist nearby?'

She gave me directions and I hurried to tell my father I'd be gone for fifteen minutes.

The chemist had a small selection of bottles. I chose one with a red furry cover and fumbled for money. I felt panicky, as if I must get this back to my mother as soon as possible; it was a matter of urgency to relieve her discomfort in whatever small way I could. I ran up the stairs at the hospital and found the nurse I'd spoken to in a sluice room. She filled the hot-water bottle and pushed the extra air out, securing it tightly. I was relieved that she seemed capable and compassionate.

'Are you on duty on my mother's ward during the night?' I asked.

'I am. I'll see to it for her.'

I sped to my mother and slid the bottle between her feet.

'How's that?' I asked anxiously.

'Grand. Ye're an angel.'

'When it gets cold, ask the nurse with the blonde hair in plaits to refill it. That's the secret of being in hospital, learn who your allies are.'

A shadow of pain crossed her face. 'I feel a bit sick,' she said. 'It's that butcher downstairs, hauling me around.'

'Have a boiled sweet,' my father suggested, 'the sugar might help.'

'Just half one.'

He bit one and gave her a sticky portion. She moved it around in her mouth, disinterested. I thought, I'd give anything to have her demand ham and chicken with cold roast spuds and send us running around trying to find goat's milk.

At ten o'clock my father and I drove back to the cottage in silence. He took himself to bed as soon as we got in, grey with pain and worry. I knew that I would hear him moving about again by three in the morning, filling the kettle and coughing his dry smoker's cough.

I got a fire going and sat by it for a while, then dialled my brother's number in Hong Kong. It would be about seven in the morning there, a reasonable hour. The last time I'd seen him was when we happened to visit at the same time five years previously. He had been here when I arrived, leaving two days later. I had felt awkward around him, not knowing enough about his life to converse easily. I was ignorant of the banking world which fascinated him and about which he talked constantly to my father. I had never met his wife or two sons; in photographs they looked handsome. He was an outsider who went his own way and seemed keen to put continents between himself and his origins. From listening to him I gathered that he was highly successful and proud of it, and of the fact that he'd climbed the ladder without much formal education. He never asked me about my job, except to enquire what I earned and congratulate me for getting out of the NHS and into a private clinic. Sometimes I actually forgot that I had a brother and found that people who'd known me for years exclaimed in surprise when I mentioned him in passing. At other times, when I was feeling low or witnessed friends enjoying the company of their siblings, I found myself wishing that I had a brother and then recalled with a start that I did.

When he answered the phone I explained that I was in Ireland and that our mother was in hospital, very ill. I wanted to say that she was dying but you have to know someone well to be that honest.

'It's for real, she's really ill?' he asked. He had picked up a faint Australian twang along the way which sat on top of his Tottenham vowels.

'Yes, it's for real. They're doing tests and it doesn't look good. I'd get here soon if I were you.'

'Oh. Okay. How's the old man?'

'Tired, stressed. She's been playing him up.'

'Tell me about it. I'll book a flight a.s.a.p.'

I put the phone down, feeling hollow and slightly nauseous. I remembered that I hadn't eaten since my snack on the plane. The flight seemed like it had happened days ago, something I'd dreamed. I made a pot of tea and some toast and ate by the fire with a tray on my lap. My mother's foul-smelling tube of unguent for aches and pains was lying on the mentelpiece, a yellowing dribble oozing from the cap. I'd bought her odour-free gels that were just as effective, but she swore by her creamy ointment that reeked of camphor and irritated the eyes at fifty paces. She was also convinced of the efficacy of salt bags for removing rheumatic aches. It wasn't unusual to walk in and find her with a home-made muslin sack containing sea salt strapped to the back of her neck or knee with a linen napkin – one of a set she'd bought from Snakey Tongue in 1964. She was keen on binding and bandaging; when her left knee was giving her gyp she tightened a thick leather strap that looked as if it originally would have been part of a horse's harness around it. When she walked, the leather creaked and the buckle jangled, causing passersby to look around, startled.

Her *pièce de résistance* in the self-medicating stakes was the invention of the hot-water bottle hat circa 1977. It was a particularly cold winter and she caught a flu that left her with sinus headaches which could only be alleviated by warmth. When she was well enough to venture out she came back saying bad cess to the blasted weather, she'd never survive the winter if this carried on. She disappeared upstairs for an afternoon and appeared triumphantly at tea time, wearing the kind of fluffy woollen beret she favoured, but one that sat strangely high on her head, as if she was a Rastafarian with curled up dreadlocks. Removing the beret, she revealed a round brass hot-water bottle with the stopper like a belly-button in its middle. She had constructed a little nest for it in the beret, securing it with strips of old flannelette sheet sown in with her big stitches. It could be eased from its nest to be re-filled. It was grand, she said, gorgeous and warm; now she'd be as toasty as old Nick himself when she went out. She made my father try it on and he pulled silly faces, putting his hands on his hips, pretending to be a model. I skulked away, picturing my friends or their mothers meeting her in the High Street and being transfixed by the pudding-shaped growth on her head. Luckily, the invention proved unsatisfactory, the brass bottle exhibiting a tendency to lurch to one side and perch like a bulging tumour over her right ear. The contraption was donated to the cat and her six newly-born kittens, giving their cardboard box central heating.

I kicked off my trainers and stretched my bare feet in front of the glowing fire. I hoped that my mother's were warm now and that the high bed wasn't too hard on her tender bones.

I thought of her there, alone amongst strangers and the picture became one of a timid young girl arriving at a big house where she knew no one and being shown to a bare, chilly attic room.

I put my cup down and listened. A hawthorn branch scratched at the window, but otherwise the silence that she had longed for in London blanketed the valley. The house felt wrong, unbalanced, the way the house in Tottenham had felt when my father was having the operation on his elbow. My mother had roamed from room to room, ill at ease, reminding me of a restless pacing tiger in the zoo.

What will he do without her? I thought. He hadn't yet realized that she was dying. Before he went to bed he'd said that as soon as the doctors sorted her out we must get her home and feed her up; a few good helpings of spuds were what she needed. I'd always assumed that he'd go before her, because of his arthritis and the powerful combination of anal-gesics and steroids he took daily, and also because men usually predeceased their wives. Knowing that she would be terrified of being alone in this remote cottage I'd imagined with great trepidation that I would ask her if she'd like to come and live with me in London. She would jump at the chance, I'd thought with a traitorous heart. After my divorce six years previously she had alluded to the space I must now have, commenting that whichever one of them went first, it was comforting to know I'd be able to put the other one up.

I'd visualized the whole awful scene, playing it over to myself many times; my vegetarian house filled with meaty smells, the cooker spattered with grease from frying, the rooms gradually filling with tat as she resumed her old acquaintanceships in Haringey and Archway, the awful possibility that she would produce nearly-new clothes for me straight from the early eighties. I would come home to find furniture moved or covered in cloths embroidered with women in crinolines gath-ering violets, terrible oil-paintings of religious scenes or ships in storm-tossed waters hammered to the walls, religious icons with votive candles perched on my bookshelves. Friends who visited would be subjected to Bridie Gallagher songs or stories about my mother's youth which they would be unable to comprehend because of her thick accent and lack of teeth. The pictures I conjured up made my scalp tighten in the old familiar way and brought back all those hours of seething frustration I had spent in her company before I escaped to university. I imagined myself regressing to a mutinous, powerless child. Now I knew that I'd been let off the hook, and I felt an icy blast of guilt because that knowledge brought relief.

My father was snoring in their bedroom across the passage, rumblings punctuated by whistling breaths. What was missing was the crackling of my mother's little transistor radio, a cheap item she'd bought in Walthamstow market. She kept it on low all night, not quite tuned in so that there were buzzings and static accompanying the Irish music. My father's poor hearing meant that he wasn't troubled by it, but I had had to buy ear plugs because the tinny racket had kept me awake. I had laughed the first night I poked the sponge aids into my ears, thinking that my mother had a talent for reversing roles; wasn't it the younger generation who were supposed to bother their elders with noise and music in the small hours? The radio was still in there, standing silent beside her bottle of Lourdes water and tin of lemon drops. She couldn't be bothered taking it to the hospital with her, she'd said listlessly and I had touched it, thinking: she is letting go the things of this world.

Nowadays, my mother's family would be called dysfunctional. She referred to them as 'the quare crew', citing their odd traits and characteristics with critical exactness, as if she had no strange quirks of her own.

They had all emigrated to England and gone their various ways with negligible contact. My mother hardly ever spoke about her brothers and sisters, didn't even know where her youngest brother lived. I had picked up the knowledge I possessed of them randomly; listening to my parents talking, my mother referring to the odd letter or overhearing her confide a family detail to a priest. Occasionally, if I slipped a question in when she was feeling talkative she'd fit another piece of the jigsaw for me. She always portrayed her own mother as a saintly woman, a hard worker with a heart of gold, but I had found her remote, her rare touch uninterested. I would wonder why, if she was such a paragon, all her children had left her, rarely visited her – apart from my mother – and pursued their adult lives imbued with a certain degree of chaos. My father had only one brother who had inherited the farm in Waterford; to me, he and his family didn't count as real kin because they had stayed in Ireland and we didn't visit them, we went to my grandmother in Bantry.

Growing up in Tottenham I was surrounded by children who had close-knit families. My friends would come to school talking about the presents they'd had from aunts and uncles for their birthdays, family trips and holidays taken with cousins, celebratory family occasions. I would listen with envy and a sense of displacement, unable to reveal that I did have aunts, uncles and cousins, but I didn't see them because they had been adopted or gone missing or because there was no contact. It all seemed somehow shameful in comparison to my friends' wholesome networks. I sensed that certain markers were missing in my life, a wider safety net of relations who would have contributed to my identity and of whom I had been deprived. It added to my feeling of not quite belonging. I saw the lack of family bond reflected in my relationship with my brother and puzzled over this absence; was it part of the losses brought about by emigration, leaving ties of country and culture? Perhaps being dispersed without points of reference caused a rift that couldn't be made whole again and this rift was passed on to children with their genetic inheritance.

Nellie, the eldest in my mother's family, had produced three illegitimate children. The youngest was born when she was only fifteen; at seventeen she ran off to Liverpool. The children were adopted and never heard of again. It struck me that three was more than misfortunate and when we visited Nellie just the once in her Liverpool house I stared at her, trying to visualize a wild-haired colleen in a permanent state of excitement. She had married a steady Englishman called Wilf who was twenty years older than her. He worked, oddly enough, for the Post Office, but behind a counter. They had no children and she treated him as if he was a spoiled son rather than a husband. He was allowed to sit in front of the TV to have his dinner which she delivered to him on a tray with a bottle of stout. We were fed chops, greens and mashed potatoes, but Wilf was apportioned chips and a fried egg with his chop because that was his favourite. For pudding we had gooseberry pie and cream; Wilf slurped pink packet whip and ice-cream, switching channels like an infant who gets easily bored. Nellie at that time would have been in her late forties, a trim woman with tortoiseshell glasses and neat movements. Her house was spotless, bare compared to ours and she cleared away after we'd eaten with great speed. I found myself wondering what it would be like to have her as a mother; I could see myself living in this normal-looking home with polished surfaces and no obvious medications.

We had only visited because my mother was attending a special mass at the new Liverpool cathedral. She had won a place at the women's-only celebration when the parish priest had drawn her name from a hat in the presbytery after benediction. She was dead set on going, even though it meant a dreaded journey, because she had entered our names in the book of the Sacred Heart that was kept on the altar and more importantly, although not acknowledged, because her arch-enemy from The Catholic Women's Guild, one Assumpta Flanagan, would be there. My mother had no intention of letting Assumpta steal a march on her by racing ahead in the holier-than-thou stakes. My father and I had to loiter around the city centre while she and Assumpta out-prayed each other and brayed the hymns competitively. My mother was hoarse, hot but triumphant as she swaggered through the cathedral doors, ready for her dinner at Nellie's.

She quizzed Nellie about her parish priest, whether or not there was a convent locally and the laying of the foundation stone of the cathedral, sniffing out her sister's lack of up-to-date information. When we left the house my mother remarked darkly on her apparent paucity of knowledge of the new place of worship, commenting on the awfulness of mixed marriages; wouldn't anyone with sense know that her wedding a Protestant old enough to be her father could cause nothing but grief. Sure there hadn't been one religious picture in the house, she'd said, crossing herself; that one was no more practising her faith than the Pope was turning Jew. The lack of bleeding hearts and po-faced statues had been a definite plus for me, making the sitting-room alluring. That was my only sighting of Nellie; like two of the other siblings, she didn't attend her mother's funeral and we heard that she'd died in 1985.

Jack, born eighteen months after Nellie, was a mystery man. He'd done a vanishing act after leaving his wife and two young children in 1940. There was talk of a gambling debt and a vengeful card sharp in what passed for the Cork underworld at the time. It was believed that Jack had nipped off on the night-boat to Swansea and rumour had it that he might have been killed in the blitz. My mother had one photo of him, a dark-haired good-looking charmer. I had his eyes and the same shape chin. In Cork he had worked in the building trade and sometimes, as I passed building sites in London, I would look at men's faces, searching for a resemblance. I once heard Nancy, his abandoned wife, tell my mother that she still loved him and during more romantic phases of adolescence I would search faces even more keenly, thrilled by the thought that I might discover him, solve the mystery of his life and return him to the bosom of his family. Whenever there were famous disappearances, stories in the paper about Lord Lucan or a vanishing businessman or MP, I would wonder about Jack; had he maybe sailed on to Australia or America, or was he sitting lonely in a lodgings in Kilburn, wanting to go home but unable to find a way? Although I'd never known him, I felt that I missed him, he was an uncle to whom I'd lost my entitlement.

John-Jo was five years younger than my mother and I thought perhaps she'd been fond of him years ago. She'd looked after him for a while when her mother was sick and had been allowed to take him to one of the houses she worked at for a couple of weeks. He lived we didn't know where and was a drinker; feckless, my mother said. I saw him once, at my grandmother's funeral, in a scene that was reminiscent of a Mike Leigh film. My father, mother, brother and myself were standing by the grave with the priest and a family called the Donavans who had been close to my grandmother. As the priest sprinkled holy water down on to the coffin, a portly middle-aged man with a high colour and a scruffy suit staggered forwards, crying, 'Mammy! Mammy!' He threw himself at the edge of the grave, hands clawing at the earth. My father and Mr Donavan tussled with him, their black ties snapping in the breeze while the priest held his hand to his mouth and

I gaped, glancing at my brother and mouthing, 'Who is *he*?' My brother shrugged and glanced at his watch. My mother kept her head bent, fingering her rosary beads.

I heard my father talking in low tones to the sobbing shape. 'Come on now, man, for God's sake and don't be making a holy show of yourself. Think of your poor mother looking down on this.'

Finally they managed to stand him up. His hair was plastered to his face with tears, snot hung from his nose and his brown shiny suit was clogged with damp earth. His shape could be seen outlined in the soil like a diagram at the scene of a crime. He shrugged them off, arms flailing wildly for a moment so that I thought he might topple backwards into the grave, then balanced himself and staggered past me. The reek of spirits made me catch my breath. We watched him totter out to the road and get into a car with a blonde woman at the wheel. She gunned the engine and they drove off. He had appeared from nowhere and vanished back there. In my grandmother's house afterwards my mother plied Mrs Donavan with cold meats and imprecations against the intruder.

'Bad cess to him anyway. To think me own brother would make a show of me like that and after all I did for him. And that ould one he was with must be the gay divorcée he's hitched to. She's an ould lush too from what I hear. May the devil take them.'

Mrs Donavan munched thoughtfully, wisely keeping quiet. This was the only clue I was given that I'd just met my uncle John-Jo. I sidled up to my father who was washing his mud-caked hands in a bowl.

'I gather that was John-Jo,' I whispered.

He glanced back to my mother, frowning. 'Don't be mentioning him now, he's a *persona non grata* if ever there was one. God knows what stone he crawled out from under but I'll tell you something, his liver must be well pickled.'

Biddy, the last in the family, lived in Southend. She and my mother exchanged letters a couple of times a year. Biddy had

60

also had an illegitimate child who had been adopted in Cork before she set sail for England. She had trained as a secretary and married Roy, a native Southender who had his own electrical business. Roy found favour with my mother because he was a Catholic – albeit an English one and therefore not one hundred per cent the real article – and extremely oily in his manner towards her. She viewed this as his natural gentlemanly quality but I think the man was terrified of her. They had one son, Danny and a daughter, May who were the only cousins I had met, three times in all. Relations with Biddy were the warmest, although in comparison to other families they bordered on deep frozen. Southend was just twenty-five miles away but it might as well have been hundreds; there were only three personal contacts that I could remember, once when we went to the coast for the day, once when they visited the city to see the Tower of London and the last, catastrophic meeting at May's wedding which had severed all communication from 1968 to the present time.

I was thrilled when we received the silver embossed wedding invitation; this was the kind of occasion proper families gathered for. It would be satisfying to be part of the usual run of things. I'd be able to mention it at school and add that May and her husband were going to Majorca for their honeymoon.

'Eoh,' my mother said in her mock posh voice when she read it over Saturday breakfast, 'how grand. Sounds too good for the likes of us!' She shoved it to my father, leaving a marmalade trail on the edge. He held it away from himself, looking nervy. 'Good enough for May, I suppose.'

I waited on tenterhooks to see if we would be going. My mother, I knew, had views about Biddy being a social climber. She and Roy had a thirties-style semi-detached with a long garden and had themselves been on a package holiday to the Costa del Sol the previous year. We'd had a postcard with an x marking their hotel room and my mother had said she didn't know what all this malarkey about the Costapacket meant, wasn't Ireland good enough for a holiday for people who didn't have their ould snouts stuck in the air? Ireland at least had proper toilets; in them ould continental places they wee-weed in the gutters.

My father passed the invite to me, saying nothing; he was always content to maintain the line of least resistance.

'Oh look,' I said lightly, pointing to the little note Biddy had included. 'A Monsignor is going to conduct the service, someone Roy knew at school.' I reckoned that the odds were for us going as soon as I'd read that. A Monsignor was high up in the church's chain of command and clergy groupie that she was, my mother would hardly be able to resist the lure of being able to fawn around him.

'Let me see,' she said, whipping it from my hand. ' "Monsignor Curran will say the mass at St Thomas's and come to the reception". Well, crikey O'Reilly! They must have a hot-line to the Vatican; I suppose a plain ould priest wouldn't be good enough for the likes of Biddy. 'Tis a pity she doesn't give me back the tenner I lent her before she throws money away on a swank reception.'

This was another bone of contention; my mother had sent Biddy a ten pound note when she'd first got a room in Kilburn and was hard up. Maybe Biddy had thought it was a gift; whatever the reason, she'd never paid it back. I poured more tea while my mother read the bit about the Monsignor again; she would be picturing his red biretta and the sash at his waist, seeing herself beside him in a group photo that she'd be able to prop on the mantelpiece when the parish priest called.

'I'm surprised the reception's at the house,' she said. 'I'd have thought they'd be booking the Grand Hotel at least.'

'Ah well now, they're not millionaires,' my father pointed out.

'The way Biddy goes on, you'd think Roy was Jean Paul Getty. Well, I suppose we'd better go; she is me youngest sister and me mother would want it.'

I swallowed a laugh with my toast and wondered if I'd be able to get a candy-striped jacket from C & A, like the one

Herman of Herman and The Hermits had been wearing on *Top of the Pops.*

My mother dragged my father to Oxford Street on four successive Saturdays before the wedding, trying to find an outfit that wasn't too tight, too long, too garish or too finicky round the neck. Buying clothes for a sixteen-and-a-half stone woman wasn't easy; my father returned from the first three trips looking grey and years older. At a low ebb he handed me twenty pounds and I zipped to Ilford and bought my candy-striped jacket with purple trousers to match. Finally my mother came home with a two-piece flowery outfit in rayon, covered in a pattern of orange, pink and yellow blossoms.

Our car was in the garage, having dramatically failed its MOT, so we were travelling by train from Liverpool Street. My mother struggled into her corset and the flowery two-piece, smoothed on her orange face powder and stuck her teeth in. She resembled a moving garden border. Her whiter-than-white dentures sparkled in the middle of her face. Her complexion was startling; orange and rosy, her blood pushed upwards by the constraining corset. I was told that I looked like something out of a circus and I sat at the other end of the platform, plotting how I would lose myself at the reception and stay as far away from her as possible.

The train was late. My mother paced up and down, muttering that she should have bought shoes in a broader fitting and swinging her handbag impatiently. My father concentrated on the timetable and chatted to the ticket inspector about how well the flowering tubs were doing.

On the train, sitting down, the corset pinched even tighter and my mother squirmed around trying to get comfortable. I hid behind my book, but just after Romford we had to move seats because my mother alleged that an ould one sitting further up the carriage and done up like a dog's dinner was ogling my father.

'Brazen as brass with a skirt up to her ass and ye a man in yeer fifties,' she said as we relocated.

63

'Sure, she was only looking down the carriage. The woman's probably short-sighted,' my father said wearily.

'I saw her fluttering her eyelashes and smiling at ye,' my mother stated. 'That hair came out of a bottle as sure as eggs is eggs. That one's out for what she can get, I'm telling ye. What would ye know, sure, ye're an innocent? All ye're ever thinking about is yeer geraniums.'

I studied my father with his grey suit, thinning hair and faraway eyes, trying and failing to see him as a desirable sexpot. Could this be a man who wandered through life scattering alluring hormones, unaware that libidinous women were panting after him, driven crazy at the sight of his St Vincent de Paul badge? Having dealt with the brazen as brass threat my mother settled back, snaffled liquorice allsorts from her bag and gave a running commentary on the state of the back gardens we passed.

At the reception I found Danny, who was a year younger than me but interested in my clothes and the latest news from swinging London. He seemed to think that I spent all my time on Carnaby Street and the King's Road and I played up to this, fabricating a hectic social life. From the corner of my eye I could see that my mother had cornered the Monsignor and was demanding his attention like an eager puppy. She seized his ring and kissed it and would probably have fallen to her knees if there hadn't been such a crush.

Biddy's house was affluent; she had leather furniture and a TV built into a special case. A woman dressed in a maid's outfit was handing around plates of little biscuits on doily-coated trays. Biddy herself looked younger than her years; like Nellie she was trim and her hair had brunette tints. She was wearing a plain blue shift dress and a string of pearls; I thought she resembled Jackie Kennedy. On the wall in the wide hallway there were photos of her and Roy with their faces grinning through cut-out matadors' shapes, a souvenir of their Spanish trip. Once again, I found myself wishing that I had a different mother. Biddy would have done nicely; she seemed organized and jolly and was polite to the Monsignor without any Uriah Heep behaviour. I didn't think she would make allegations about strangers on public transport. When I asked, Danny assured me that she never went to second-hand shops.

Danny wanted to show me his dog, which had been banished to the shed outside while the reception was on. We had to move past my mother on our way out. Biddy was talking to her, patting her arm confidingly.

'Oh, there's nothing like extra weight to make a woman look older,' she was saying. 'I go to a health place to keep trim and I watch my diet. If you like I'll give you my tips sheet. I know it's a struggle in middle age.'

My mother was looking ill-tempered and puffy but the Monsignor was standing nearby so I was confident that she would stay on her best behaviour. Danny and I took the dog out for a walk, eating our vol-au-vents and thin prawn sandwiches as we went along. I thought, here I am, out with my cousin on a fine day and I had a warm feeling of sheer normality. This was a scene that matched the stories I'd grown up on; ones that featured confident middle-class children with comfortable houses and mothers healthily free of neuroses, mothers who were caring in a low-key way, efficient and calm, dedicated to keeping their houses spotless and capable of rustling up a picnic or arranging an outing at the drop of a hat. Most importantly of all, mothers who *fitted in* and didn't draw attention to themselves. My deep-seated conviction that this should have been my birthright expanded in the July sun and by the time we turned back into Danny's street I was day-dreaming a plan which would have me moving to Southend and taking up residence in the spare room next to May's.

I was hurtled back to reality by Danny shaking my arm and pointing. Outside his house stood my parents, my father clutching his trilby to his chest, my mother wagging a finger at Biddy who was gripping the gate with rigid knuckles. As we drew nearer my mother's voice rang strongly, ricocheting around the quiet suburban street.

'... ye can stuff yeer ould wedding and yeer ould trifles, ye tight-fisted jade. I'm a martyr to me nerves but I tried to lend a Christian hand and what thanks did I get? I wouldn't come back here if ye begged me on bended knees, so I wouldn't!'

I froze against a fence a few doors away, Danny beside me, the dog growling softly. Curtains were twitching and a door behind us creaked open an inch. Roy was silhouetted in the shaded hallway of the house, his hands clasped before his face, two forefingers pressed to his lips.

'Kitty, I'm sure we can sort things out if you'll just step back in,' Biddy said softly.

'Oh, I'm not staying here to be insulted like a slip of a kitchen girl. I know when I'm not good enough. I was good enough for a tenner when ye didn't have a penny to yeer name, though! The likes of ye always have money. Come on!' She pushed my father and beckoned to me.

I looked away as I passed Biddy and followed them along the street. We left behind us a heavy silence that I can still hear along the years.

The station was a hot fifteen minutes' walk. My mother sped ahead, puffing, my father a couple of steps behind her. No words were exchanged. At the station she disappeared to the Ladies. I found that I was shivering.

'What was that about?' I asked my father.

He shook his head. 'Some sort of set-to in the kitchen. Your mother went to help Biddy and after ten minutes she came driving through saying she'd been accused of ruining the trifles.'

'How?'

'God knows, son, God knows. Just keep your head down till it blows over.'

When my mother came back I could tell she'd taken off her corset and stuffed it in her bag; her flesh was now free-moving, her skirt straining at the zip. She bought me a chocolate bar I didn't want from a machine and handed it to me saying,

'Take warning from what happened back there; yeer own flesh and blood can turn on ye.'

At that moment I hated her passionately. I wanted her to die, I wanted to cut her suffocating presence out of my life. Just standing there, looming broadly in front of me, she blocked my light.

The chocolate melted in my pocket on the journey back, staining my jacket. I hadn't said goodbye to Danny and that was the last time I saw him. He died suddenly of a brain haemorrhage in his late twenties. There were no more letters or Christmas cards exchanged between Tottenham and Southend.

FIVE

My brother arrived, looking tanned but tired, three days after I'd called him. He had hired his own car at the airport and I heard him drive in fast through the gate, scattering hens before him.

'It's Mr time-means-money,' my father said, rolling a cigarette. This was how he always referred to my brother, although never in front of him. My mother didn't like the nickname and would tut crossly. I wondered what they called me in my absence and whether my brother knew.

We shook hands as he took a case from the car boot.

'How is she?' he asked.

'About the same. They're doing a biopsy today and should be able to tell us something definite after that. Dad's inside.'

He yawned. 'I'm jet-lagged. Need a hot bath.'

He and my father nodded a greeting to each other and my brother handed him a pack of duty-free tobacco. My father gave me a sly look; I always refused to provide him with tobacco because it had dire effects on his chest.

It was agreed that my brother and I would go to the hospital during the afternoon, leaving my father the evening visit for himself. After Dermot had bathed and had a bite to eat we set off in his car.

'They should never have moved back here,' he said, lighting up a long slim cigarette. 'She's never been happy.'

68

'Where would she be happy? Have you ever known her happy?'

I genuinely wanted to discover if he had; I harboured an idea that because he had grown up with a younger mother she might also have been a different one, a slimmer, carefree zestful woman.

There was a silence. 'She was better in London, had more to distract her.'

'She was the one who pushed to live here.'

'She likes the going but not the getting there. She's always been subject to peculiar moods. I remember her crying for no reason. Did you know her grandfather committed suicide?'

I looked at him through the coiling blue cigarette smoke. 'No. Which grandfather?'

'Her father's father. He drowned himself in one of the Dublin canals.'

'How do you know that?'

'She told me once. He was an oddball, took himself off to live like a hermit, built himself a shack they called a "cuddy" in the glens near the house. He'd pop up now and again for a shave and a good feed, then go back to his solitary life. One of his brothers was the same and ended his days in the loony bin. She said she reckoned her family had melancholy blood and it was coming out in her.'

Rain was sweeping in across the fields. I rubbed a patch of condensation on my window. 'Blood will out' had always been one of her favourite sayings. Had she spent much of her life terrified of the potential for disaster that flowed in her veins? Maybe she had taken all those medicines as a preventive, holding fate at bay.

Dermot opened his window and threw his cigarette butt out. 'She had a theory that her brother Jack had topped himself in London, or maybe jumped overboard during the night-crossing. He took nothing with him when he left home.'

'Was he depressed?'

'His wife – what's her name?'

'Nancy.'

'That's right. Nancy said he hadn't slept for weeks before he took off. That's a sign of depression, isn't it?'

'Can be.' Unexpected layers were being revealed. All those times I'd looked out for Jack and he may have been fish-food years ago.

Dermot switched to talking about his bank and I watched the rain drowning the land. As we drew up at the hospital I decided to snatch a rare chance for information.

'Did she ever tell you what happened to the trifles at May's wedding?' I asked him.

He stared. 'What trifles?'

'Nothing. I thought you might know why she'd quarrelled with Biddy.'

'No, she never said.'

She was lying back on the pillow with her eyes closed, a hand tucked under her chin. I shook her arm gently and she looked up.

'Ah, Dermot,' she said, 'I knew ye'd come, I knew it.'

'Sure I did. How're you doing?'

'Oh, not good. They took a bit of me liver away this morning. I'm terrible sore.'

'Still, they need to find out what's wrong.'

'That's what Rory said, that's why he put me in here.'

'I've brought some yogurt,' I told her.

She nodded. 'I've no appetite.'

She lapsed into a silence, staring to her side. Dermot reached up and switched the hospital radio on.

'Have a bit of music, it cheers the place up.'

We sat, listening to a pop song. I found it grating, unnecessary. She seemed unaware of it.

'Will ye get me some grapefruit juice from the shop below?' she asked me.

I left them to go and buy it. While I was at the shop I picked up an English paper, thinking that they would like some time alone. Dermot had to fly back in forty-eight hours.

I sat on a window ledge, reading. There was an obituary for a Hollywood star who had died, but when I saw that it had been of cancer I turned the page. My parents had bought Irish papers in London; the *Cork Examiner*, the *Dungarvan Herald*, *Ireland's Own*. My mother would turn to the back pages of the *Cork Examiner*, immediately looking to see who had died. That was the only section that interested her. She spent hours mulling over the columns, jabbing her finger at well-known names, wondering aloud about others who she thought she remembered, speculating about causes of death; 'Wasn't he the fella who lived up around Brian's Bridge and had the wife who fell into the quarry; she had every bone in her body crushed and was the cousin of the one who sold the mother's horse to the tinkers. I wonder, did he die of a thrombosis like his ould one?' Once she saw the name of her meanest employer, the one from whom she'd stolen the marmalade, and gave a crow of laughter, saying she hoped she'd gone to the hot place and was being tormented by divils with pokers.

She was attracted by death, the ways in which people met it and the forms of their funerals. She sometimes attended the funeral masses and burials of people she had barely known or not known at all, watching out for the services advertised in the parishes around us. She would slip into the back of the church, attaching herself to the cortège afterwards. No one ever questioned her, probably because she played the part of the grieving mourner so well. She had a second-hand funeral outfit, a swanky D. H. Evans black suit, plain with a purple trim on the collar. Her head was covered by a black lace mantilla which imparted a vague look of celebrity; she would keep it bowed reverently, rosary beads twined in her fingers.

On one occasion when she was lured further afield, to Twickenham, she took me with her; it must have been a school holiday. She had read a newspaper report about a lonely old woman, originally a native of Galway, she was in her late eighties and had been murdered in her bed for the two hundred pounds she kept under the mattress. The local priest was interviewed, expressing his shock, regret, etc; Mary Quinlan had had no family in England and had never been married. My mother deduced correctly that Mary would have few to mourn her passing and decided that she had a duty to bolster the numbers. She donned her D. H. Evans outfit, dressed me in a black Little Lord Fauntleroy jacket from Sue Ryder and we embarked on a long bus journey. There were four mourners: us, the priest and an altar boy. I wondered if Mary Quinlan had been a recluse or a horrible woman no one liked. It was the first funeral I'd been to and I found it disappointing; no choir, no music, no pomp and ceremony, just the priest's droning voice, the lacklustre warbling of the altar boy and a cheap-looking coffin. I pictured the figure in there. I knew that she had been stabbed to death and I tried to puzzle out if the body would still be bleeding, but decided that it couldn't be because there were no red stains on the coffin. My mother belted out the responses, her rosary beads clicking ten to the dozen, determined to give Mary a decent send-off. The undertaker let us ride to the cemetery behind the hearse, assuming that we were kin. I was impressed with the size of the car and its gleaming bodywork. After the interment the priest enquired how we were related to the deceased and when my mother said oh not at all, he'd got the wrong end of the stick entirely; we weren't family, just concerned Catholics, he looked taken aback, as if he'd been conned.

I folded my paper and returned to the ward. Dermot was standing outside in the corridor, puffing at a cigarette and blowing the smoke out of an open window. In between puffs he concealed the cigarette in the hollow of his hand, turning the fingers inwards. He gave me a jaundiced look as I approached and grimaced, jerking a thumb in my mother's direction.

'She got rid of you on purpose so she could work on me,' he said.

'What do you mean?'

'I got the lot; you forced her in here, she didn't want to be in hospital, I've got to help her get out. She wants to go home right now. I'm not to tell you because you'll try to stop me.'

Oh God, I thought, I can't face this. Will she ever lay off blackmailing people? Could she not stop now she's dying? I took my jumper off and loosened the collar of my shirt.

'What did you say?'

'What could I say? She started crying on me. She was trying to climb out of bed; a nurse had to help me get her back in. I ran out in the end, couldn't take it. What should I do?'

I found myself thinking; you should know what to do, you're the eldest, you should be shouldering the responsibility.

I shook my head. 'I don't know. Let me think.' I walked up and down, wishing suddenly that I smoked. 'Let's go in and talk to her together.'

He shrugged. 'Okay, but she'll be impossible.'

There were two women, other patients, at her bedside, offering her tissues and patting her hands.

'Sure stop now, pet,' one was saying, 'you'll only make things worse.'

My mother took a deep breath and bellowed with an alarming strength:

'Please, please God, let me out of here!'

When the women saw us they got up and pattered away. One of them started crying. My mother slid down in the bed, tears on her cheeks. Seeing us together, she knew that Dermot had told me.

He sat down. I stood, the bully who had imposed his will, holding the newspaper and grapefruit juice.

'You shouldn't tell Dermot I forced you in here,' I said. 'He's come a long way and you're not being fair to him.'

'The docs have got to find out what's up,' Dermot said.

'Ye're like a pair of vultures, waiting to pick at me carcass.' She reached out for Dermot's hand. 'I want to be alone with me eldest son,' she said plaintively, grasping at him and throwing me a venomous look.

73

I blinked. He won't be here to look after you when you get home, I wanted to tell her; he wasn't here to wash your hair and fetch you a bottle for your feet.

I nodded. 'I'll meet you downstairs,' I told him and turned away.

The nurse who had helped with the hot-water bottle was at the nursing station, filling out charts. She gave me a sympathetic smile and picked up a file.

'I'm glad I caught you,' she said. 'The doctor wanted me to ask you; has your mother ever had an alcohol problem?'

'Alcohol?' I repeated stupidly.

'Yes. Her liver seems to be in a bad way; we just wondered . . .'

'No, no. She doesn't drink, never has.'

The nurse made a note. 'Thanks.' She made a little gesture with her pen. 'Your mother's a bit worked up today. We had trouble persuading her to go for the biopsy, she wanted to get off the trolley.'

I pictured her, fighting them, frightened of the tests to come. All her life she had flirted with medicine and now the reality was daunting. I wanted to cry for her and spit rage at her. I couldn't speak to the nurse whose kind eyes were too much to bear. I hurried away and walked around the outskirts of the hospital. Leaves were drifting and forming little mounds. The sharpness of November air scratched my cheeks.

Sometimes, in the autumn, my mother used to take me to Hampstead Heath; we'd kick through the leaves and feed the squirrels, then she'd say that we'd go and have a gander at Kenwood House, see what the toffs had on show today. I would laugh as she mimicked someone's walk in front of us, but I was always holding part of myself in reserve in case the person turned around accusingly and she squared up to them, asking what were they gorming at and didn't they have anything better to do? She had been my entertainer and my persecutor.

Alcohol! I thought, and laughed. My mother had one glass

of sherry every Christmas which she drank with her little finger cocked, just the way she'd seen it done in the big houses. In Tottenham she used to share this rare treat with Miss Diamond, the elderly spinster lady who lived next door to us. Miss Diamond fascinated me because she had a whiskery chin and whistled as she talked. My mother made Miss Diamond her Christmas dinner; it was laid out on the best china and delivered next door by my father on a tray with a snowy napkin. Then, at ten to three Miss Diamond's tentative knock would be heard at the front door; my mother would open it and Miss Diamond's tray would appear, the china and cutlery washed and dried, followed by the lady herself. She and my mother would sit in armchairs, their sherry poised, and wait for the Queen's Christmas message which they listened to with appreciative murmurs. Every year I would sit in the background, waiting with mounting excitement to mouth the words that were always exchanged at the end of the broadcast; my mother would turn to Miss Diamond and say, 'Hasn't she a lovely voice, Miss Diamond,' and Miss Diamond would reply in her broad cockney accent, 'Yais, Mrs Keenan!' I would clutch my over-full stomach in silent laughter and succumb to hiccups.

Miss Diamond, who smelled of mouse droppings and tinned peas would then pass her Christmas present for us to my mother and my mother would return with our gift. Miss Diamond's offering to us was always a painting, executed by herself in dark, forbidding colours, of a bowl of fruit or a vase of flowers. Her initials, B. D., featured in yellow like a trace of egg yolk in the bottom right-hand corner. We always gave her embroidered handkerchiefs. The paintings were stacked year after year in the top of the airing cupboard until there must have been at least twenty of them up there. They fell on my father's head one day when he was rootling for a towel and he said he was lucky he'd kept his brain and why did we have to hang on to these bloody yokes, they looked like dead things and the colours were enough to give you the screaming

75

hab-dabs. My mother said that we should keep them in case Miss Diamond became a famous artist; then we'd be on to a fortune and laughing all the way to the bank.

I turned for the car. Dermot was walking slowly from the building, holding his coat, head bent to catch the flame from his lighter.

'Phew,' he said, 'that was something. I persuaded her to stay until they got the biopsy result.' He looked like a man who'd been through ten rounds in the ring.

'When did you say you'd be in again?'

'In the morning, then in the evening. I didn't tell her yet that I'm flying back the day after tomorrow. Better not upset her too much.'

'I'll let you and Dad visit tomorrow. I think it's best if I stay away for a bit.'

He nodded and tipped ash on to the grass. 'That hospital's a dump.'

I didn't reply; it seemed average to good to me.

'If there's any costs for nurses, things like that when she comes home, let me know,' he said, starting the car. 'Will you be around for the duration?'

'Yes, I've arranged for my job to be covered.'

Dermot stared at the road. 'She's going, isn't she?'

'Yes. She's going.'

And like all the journeys I'd made with her, this one was fraught, unpredictable and subject to swift changes.

Raising the Banner

War was waged between my mother and her arch-enemy Assumpta Flanagan for over twenty years. The battle terrain moved according to opportunities presented and quick reflexes were needed to maximize combat capabilities. Guerrilla tactics with unexpected ambushes were deployed; there were skirmishes, flank attacks, sabotage, tactical withdrawals and the occasional pitched battle.

Mrs Flanagan was a skeletally thin, dried-up-looking woman who had had her womb removed by mistake. It happened in the days before people had the confidence to sue for medical negligence; the experience had left her embittered and with a pinched expression that my mother described as looking as if she had a lemon stuck in her gob. Her husband was a small ratty-looking man with a delicate chest and permanently greasy hair who my mother referred to as the oily gom. When I had a Saturday job in the chemist's, he came in regularly for cough drops and Brylcreem but we were too embarrassed to acknowledge each other because we were trapped in the no man's land between campaigns.

Although Assumpta and my mother knew each other from church, they had first sniffed the scent of mutual enmity when they met in the factory where they worked as part-time cleaners. It was one of the many fleeting jobs my mother tried out, hoarding the money for her shopping jaunts.

The incident which had triggered the first clash was buried in the mists of time; something about a missing mop and bucket seemed to lie at the bottom of it. My mother had steamed home, claiming that that ould Flanagan jade had held her up in her work, bad cess to her, and the boss had ticked her off for not finishing an office floor. Further despatches were delivered about ripped dusters, fecked polish, banjaxed brushes and adulterated detergent.

I was once taken along to the factory for an evening sentry shift so that I could stand guard over my mother's locker; she had decided to become pro-active, declaring, ''Tis too late to sharpen the sword when the drum beats for battle,' to a startled night-watchman. There were six cleaners; they had a floor each and their own equipment. My mother posted me by the door of the cleaners' room with my orders: 'If that ould one comes near ye, holler. Tell her if she touches me things I'll melt her into an ointment.' I hovered by the grey steel lockers, reading *The Dandy* and twitching nervously every time I heard a footstep. I half-expected Mrs Flanagan to creep up and chloroform me, or perhaps send an agent to lure me away under false pretences. My imagination was fired by the empty feel of the building and the odd faint echo of a dragging bucket or vacuum cleaner. It raced into overdrive and I envisaged being taken hostage, secured with dusters and held to ransom. Every quarter of an hour, my mother would come puffing up the corridor to ask if I'd seen anything, but I had nothing to report. She would then blow some cooling air down the front of her dress and head off, warning me to stay sharp and keep my eyes peeled. I was disappointed that nothing had happened so I took a blue crayon from my pocket and made a little mark on the door of Mrs Flanagan's locker, but it wasn't noticed. When she saw me at the end of her shift Mrs Flanagan merely sniffed and made some comment about grown-ups using children to do their dirty work.

The culmination of the factory campaign came with the incident of the shoe marks. Someone had sabotaged Assumpta's clean toilet by coating a shoe sole with black polish and pressing it down on the floor tiles and up the wall by the wash basins. The crime wasn't discovered until the following morning and questions were asked at the beginning of the next evening shift.

My father and I were having a quiet leisurely tea when my mother stormed in, wrestling off her apron and the scarf she wore over her hair à la Ena Sharples. As she reported it, the Flanagan one had burst into tears and accused her, saying words that my mother couldn't possibly repeat but that she wouldn't have expected a Catholic woman to know. (She touched the edge of the crucifix on the wall as she mentioned this.) My mother, who was obviously tiring of both the job and that particular field of combat, had handed in her notice, saying grandly that she didn't have to listen to such filth; sure didn't she have a husband to support her, she had no need to go out to work at all and she'd only done it for a bit of pin money.

My father and I were relieved, hoping that the lull in hostilities might be a long one. But an hour later Mr Flanagan rapped on the door. My mother saw him through the curtain and vanished to the bathroom, leaving my father to tighten his braces and answer the knock. I hung around at the bottom of the stairs, listening and chewing my nails.

There was a nervous coughing. 'Ah, Mr Keenan, ain't it?'

'That's right.'

'I'm Des Flanagan. Listen, mate, can't you control that Mrs o' yours?'

'Now, wait a minute . . .' my father started, but Mr Flanagan had obviously built himself up to the confrontation and was eager to say his piece.

'I dunno wot's up wiv your Mrs but she's aht of order, mate; off 'er bleedin' rocker if you arsk me. She's got my Mrs in a right old state and it's not on, mate, just not on. It's gotta stop or I tell ya, I'll end up in the bleedin' nut 'ouse.'

I had the feeling that my father might like to join him there. He glanced behind to check that my mother was still upstairs and stepped forwards, pulling the door to so that I had to strain to hear.

'Look, I don't know what's been going on but why don't we both try to calm our women folk down?'

'Easier said than done, mate,' said Mr Flanagan, rubbing his chest.

'You talk to your Mrs and I'll have a word with mine. See if we can't get them to back off.' Then my father engaged in a crafty psychological ploy; 'women, eh!' he said knowingly, drawing Mr Flanagan into the male brotherhood; 'what makes them tick, who can tell?'

Mr Flanagan was hooked. 'Don't tell me abaht it!' he groaned. 'What would you do wiv 'em?'

'Ah, the age-old conundrum. Sure they're a mystery.'

'Certainly are.'

'I'll do what I can.'

'Yeah, okay. Honest though, mate, I can't take much more. She's at 'ome in tears. Couldn't even tell me wot it's abaht this time. D'you know?'

'Shoe marks in the toilet.'

'Oh. Right. You won't let me dahn?'

'I'll see to it once, you know, once she's *calmer*.'

Mr Flanagan coughed his way to the gate. My father closed the door and slumped against the hall wall, rubbing his forehead. He saw me and shook his head.

'Your mother,' he told me in a resigned voice, 'could eat me for breakfast, dinner and tea and start on Flanagan for supper.'

He took himself off to the garden and tidied sweet peas. My mother came down for a snack, looking haughty, and reminded him that he needed to cut back the wisteria. She spread fish paste on toast and watched him through the window.

'I don't need me husband to fight me battles for me,' she told me with satisfaction, 'I raise me own banner, not like some I could mention.'

I opened the cupboard under the stairs and had a look at the shoes in there but I couldn't find any missing or coated in tell-tale black.

The next outbreak of hostilities that I was aware of featured shoes again; the victory on that occasion went to Assumpta, whose usually prinked-up mouth relaxed half a centimetre. Her attack came during the annual pilgrimage to Walsingham in Norfolk, a feast of praying, hymn-singing and sermonizing dedicated to Our Lady. My mother and I had gone with a group of about thirty parishioners in a coach one Sunday morning. Assumpta was there, and to my mother's chagrin had bagged the seat at the front nearest the priest; honour dictated that we had to sit as far away from her as possible at the rear of the coach, thus depriving us of the priest's witticisms. Assumpta's tinkling laugh danced down to us. My mother got her rosary beads out, assumed a devout expression and recited a litany.

It was a baking June day and my mother's corns were giving her hell. I was going through a holy period at this stage, thinking about becoming a priest or a monk, so I was determined to ignore any discomfort caused by the heat and offer it up as proof of my suitability for a vocation in the clerical life. I was looking for a sign from the day, a nod via God's mother to confirm that I was on the right track. At Walsingham we formed up with coachloads of other pilgrims, joining the procession that would walk several miles to the shrine, behind a huge statue of Our Lady. The statue, resplendent in blue-and-white robes and with a garland of pink roses in its head, was carried on a platform by six sturdy men, Knights of Saint Columbanus. It was the custom for pilgrims to walk barefoot. I slipped off my shoes and tied them to my belt via their laces; my mother carried her sandals in her hand.

Assumpta was several rows behind us, still tagging along with the priest. We set off, the heat from the tarmac making us shuffle uncomfortably. My mother groaned as her corns objected to the rough surface but I reminded her that her suffering would be noted on her credit sheet in heaven. We sang 'Oh Queen of Heaven, the Ocean's Star', and 'Ave Maria', my mother and Assumpta attempting to out-trill each other in the still air.

Then about a mile from the shrine, the catastrophe happened. One of the Knights, overcome by the heat, the weight of the statue and his constricting sash of honour, stumbled, lost his footing and in going down, tripped the Knight behind. There were cries from the front; we saw the high statue waver, tip from side to side, its rose crown flying into the hedge, then fall from sight. The cries turned to shouts and white plaster sprayed into the air.

'Our Lady!' my mother gasped, 'Our Lady's hurt!'

She darted out of line and disappeared up the side of the road towards the injured Madonna. I followed her, breaking into a run. The statue was in several dozen pieces, one of its outstretched arms lying across the neck of the unconscious Knight who had caused the accident. There was mayhem for some time, while the statue was cleared from the road and the Knights were sorted out. One had sprained his ankle in falling and another had been hit in the chest by a carrying pole; there was a suspected cracked rib. An ambulance was called and by the time the dregs of the procession were ready to carry on, an hour had passed. My mother had been helping to collect fragments of the statue, kissing each piece before she added it to the plaster pile. As we re-formed our ranks for the procession she looked around and then at me.

'Where's me sandals?'

'I don't know. You were carrying them.'

'I must have thrown them down by the side of the road. Help me look for them.'

The procession set off as we went back over our tracks, searching the verges. The sandals were nowhere to be seen.

'Sweet Jesus on high take pity on me,' my mother said. 'They're gone. Me feet'll be in ribbons. Someone must have took them.' She contemplated her sweating feet and then flicked her thumb against her forefinger.

'What was that Flanagan one doing all the time I was helping with Our Lady?'

I shook my head. 'No idea, I didn't see her.'

'That jade's taken them, I bet me bottom dollar. She's probably hiked them into a field or buried them. Lord God, I'll melt her so I will. I'll have her jelly guts for garters!'

We set off after the pilgrims who had vanished, my mother grimacing as her feet struck the road in the noon heat. Near the shrine we caught up with them and my mother made a bee-line for Assumpta who was clasping one of the roses from Our Lady's crown to her scrawny breast.

'Come here to me,' my mother said, pushing her on the shoulder. 'What have ye done with me sandals?'

Assumpta stepped back. 'What are you talking about, Mrs Keenan?'

'Don't ye Mrs Keenan me! Ye know what I'm talking about, ye jade ye. Ye've made off with me sandals.'

Assumpta sniffed at the rose. 'I've no idea what you're going on about. I expect you've put them down somewhere.'

'Yes, like I put me duster down in the typing room and when I came back from relieving meself 'twas gone!'

People were turning and looking disapprovingly. I moved behind a shrub and pressed my nose into its foliage. It smelled like cat's pee. Our parish priest hurried over to my mother and asked what seemed to be the problem? My mother launched into a heated explanation while Assumpta looked cool and disdainful. These were canny tactics and timing on Assumpta's part; the priest who had departed the parish a couple of months previously, Father Corcoran, had been my mother's crony. He was a man in his fifties from Donegal who liked his food and the horses. He called regularly at our house to knock back porter cake and bottled Guinness while he and my mother sat cracking jokes by the fire and jawing about the old days in the Emerald Isle. His replacement, Father Berry, was a sober, intense young man from Colchester who only paid home visits if his parishioners were sick or dying. Cultivating menopausal middle-aged ladies was not his forte.

'But it's such an odd allegation to make, Mrs Keenan,' he said, in his nasal tones, 'you've no proof at all.'

'I know what I know,' my mother gulped, 'I know she's taken them.'

'Really, Father,' said Assumpta, 'I think Mrs Keenan must be suffering heat stroke.'

'Ask her about me missing duster,' my mother said wildly.

Father Berry looked pained. 'You do seem very hot, Mrs Keenan,' he said. 'Come into the chapel and sit down; it's cooler in there. Maybe it will help get things in perspective.'

'D'ye mean ye're not going to do anything about it?' demanded my mother. 'How am I to get home without me sandals?'

'We'll think of something,' the priest advised, looking sterner. 'Now I must insist that we move inside. People have already had a terrible shock with the accident and it isn't seemly for ladies to be squabbling like this on a holy day.' He gestured for her to enter the chapel.

I had rarely seen my mother lost for words but she was then; she couldn't disobey a man of the cloth and he was obviously giving her no quarter. As she plodded into the shadow I saw the glimmer of a smile on Assumpta's lips. I had to hand it to her; she had seized an unexpected opportunity and executed her attack with guile, in the best guerrilla tradition.

I waited outside the chapel while the short service was conducted; I knew that it would seem hollow without the statue as its centrepiece. I decided that Our Lady was indicating in a dramatic fashion and at great personal inconvenience that the priesthood wasn't to be my calling; obviously God's grand plan for me sketched a different route.

Over the years, my mother and Assumpta kept careful check that they were level-pegging in holy business; like competitive traders in a spiritual stock market, they were always on the look-out for shares in the Deity. Both were members of The Catholic Women's League, The Madonna's Sodality and The Guild of Saint Teresa and subscribed postally to The Poor Boys' Appeal, which trained the said boys for priesthood in the missions. My mother edged forward on the latter front by striking up a correspondence with Father Bhattacharya, the appeal's organizer. Judging by his letters he was either very simple or very cunning because they were full of sycophantic and gushing expressions of thanks which my mother made a point of reading out aloud in the church porch, within earshot of Assumpta. The two of them made a point of attending as many masses, benedictions, holy hours and retreats as possible; you could always tell if Assumpta had missed out by the contented look on my mother's face when she came home. I think that my mother's interest in funerals started when she realized that they offered a way of increasing the number of masses she could notch up in a week; she also upped the stakes by going to other parishes, thus cannily spreading her share portfolio. My mother bested Assumpta by getting our names in the Book of the Sacred Heart first, but Assumpta beat her when she asked her cousin to have a rosary blessed for her in St Peter's by the Pope.

The battle of the flowers was the last great stand-off that I knew of before I left home. It caused my mother and Assumpta to be the unacknowledged subject of a Sunday sermon. Father Berry had foolishly allowed both of them to join the rota for arranging the church flowers; any sensible person would have realized that this was a guaranteed recipe for disaster, but the priest had a pitiful belief in his parishioners' ability to overcome their differences and pull together for the sake of the greater good.

By some dreadful irony of fate – some might have seen Satan's hand in the matter – their two names came up for decorating the church for Corpus Christi, along with a Mrs Deasy who was felled by a kidney infection three days before the event. The light of combat entered my mother's eye and her words of sympathy for Mrs Deasy rang false. She knew that she had to have her wits about her because Assumpta's sister was a florist. They had brief words about what display they should concoct; Assumpta was in favour of a single theme of massed lilies – her sister had a plentiful supply – but my mother snorted that lilies were an unmanly flower; she wanted deep-red roses, signifying the blood of Christ. My father had an allotment stocked with them and they were going cheap in the High Street. Both refused to budge; hostilities declared, they beetled away to amass their chosen blooms.

The feast day, a holy day of obligation, was on a Thursday. On the Wednesday evening my mother and Assumpta got their respective husbands to drive them to the church, the car boots swollen with flowers. They waved their spouses goodbye without any acknowledgement of each other's presence. Wordlessly, they set about snipping, trimming and arranging their lilies and roses in jugs and vases, dashing for spaces and jumbling the displays together. The church was drenched in perfume and the altar, where all eyes would focus, was swathed so heavily in flowers that the tabernacle was hardly visible. They watched each other with eagle eyes at the end; my father turned up before Mr Flanagan, but my mother wouldn't leave before Assumpta was safely in her car.

The next morning, my mother rose at six and headed off to the church, telling my father that she wanted to make some last minute adjustments and mist-spray the roses to freshen them for Our Lord. She was back at eight for breakfast, humming and making a hearty fry-up. Nine o'clock was the first mass. When the congregation arrived they witnessed an altar stacked high with roses; an extra line of them had been added since the night before, strung in a half-circle across the front of the white linen altar cloth. Lilies featured only at the back and sides of the church and they looked a little worse for wear. Assumpta took one look at the sabotage and stormed out, crossing to the presbytery and waiting for the priest to finish the service.

When he phoned my mother later in the morning, she acted the innocent saying that yes, she had reorganized the lilies because when she'd hurried to the church very early, anxious to make sure the display was looking its best, they had been drooping; maybe Mrs Flanagan hadn't realized that the blooms weren't in their first flush and would fade so quickly. Sure her sister, the florist, had probably had them in a back room for days, whereas most of the roses had only been cut the night before. She'd tried to reason with Mrs Flanagan the other day but unfortunately that lady hadn't wanted to listen.

'Sure I didn't do wrong, did I, Father?' my mother asked meekly. 'I got up at six to make sure everything was ship-shape. Ye can imagine me disappointment when I saw the lilies past their best. I thought I was doing Mrs Flanagan a favour in the heel of the hunt, but sure I know that whatever I do, she'll point the finger at me. There's some people that can't help thinking ill of their fellow men.'

Father Berry gave up. The following Sunday he preached about brotherly and sisterly love, avoiding pettiness in life and putting aside our differences in our love of Christ. My mother sat nodding in agreement.

Temporarily routed, Assumpta took herself off to mass in the next parish for several weeks, then regrouped by initiating a collection for a new mosaic for the side chapel.

Assumpta died suddenly of a thrombosis in 1972, leaving a huge gap in my mother's life; the war had been won, but victory was hollow because the enemy had beaten an unexpected final retreat. My mother attended her funeral and placed a bunch of roses by her grave.

SIX

The doctor invited my father and me into a small room near her office. I knew that my worst fears were about to be confirmed when she offered us tea.

'Your brother?' she enquired.

'He had to fly back to Hong Kong this morning,' I told her.

He had looked puzzled as I said goodbye to him, like a man who can't quite remember what he wanted to say.

'She used to be so much bigger,' he'd mused as he wiped his windscreen. 'She had a lot of life in her; she'd sing songs. Do you remember "Dear Old Skibbereen"?'

The doctor waited until my father had stirred his tea, then told us that my mother had advanced cancer of the liver; it had started in the ovaries, hence the bleeding, and then spread. It was rapid, very rapid. They would give her morphine, palliative treatment, that was all. She could come home tomorrow.

My father put his tea on the floor beside him and sat forward, head lowered, hands resting between his knees.

'How long does she have?' he asked.

'Not long; maybe a month.'

'Have you told her?' I touched my father's knee. My hand felt like lead.

'No. We didn't know what you would want.'

My father cleared his throat. 'I don't want her told. She has a horror of cancer, a horror.'

The doctor said she'd leave us for a bit and get on with making arrangements for discharge. My father put his head back against the wall and closed his eyes.

'Ah God, ah God,' he said quietly. 'Of all the ways to go . . . this.'

I sat in silence. I should have prepared him, I thought; this shouldn't have come as a shock. I cursed myself for avoiding it, but I had kept my own counsel, hoping against hope that I was wrong.

'What'll we tell her, Rory?' my father asked me. 'She knows something's up. How will we explain?'

I thought of her eyes as she had clutched at Dermot and her attempts to resist the biopsy. She knows anyway, I thought, inside herself she knows; how would you not know that you're being eaten away, that you're gradually fading, giving up? But I thought that she wouldn't want it named or to name it herself; if it had no name it would have no true claim to her.

I turned to my father. His light blue eyes, the eyes she'd always reckoned had made other women look twice, were washed with fear.

'Let's see how it goes. We'll say her liver's in a bad way. Being able to come home will distract her anyway.'

My father took out a hanky and rubbed his mouth. 'Could you go and see her? I'll just sit a while.'

I stood, knowing that I was about to start the longest walk of my life. As I opened the door I heard my father say, 'Will she make Christmas, I wonder?'

My shirt was sticking to my back in the intense hospital heat. I took a few minutes outside the ward to compose myself. This would be the first time I'd seen her since the scene with Dermot. The night after that had happened, I'd walked the lanes around the house, cursing her, dwelling on all the instances in years gone by when she had needled and embarrassed me. I was in my late twenties before I finally felt that I had stepped out of her shadow; her obsessions had held our household in thrall, my father and I standing by as spectators, an audience responding to the drama being enacted.

Angela, my ex-wife, had accused me of being like my father; emotionally illiterate. She had seen him retreat behind his book or paper when my mother was waxing lyrical. One day Angela had startled me by asking had I never considered that my mother might be the way she was because my father had such limited responses? When I pressed her to explain, she'd asked why my mother had turned her enormous energy, all her creativity, inwards, focusing on illness and depression. Then she supplied the answer; because she was married to a self-effacing man who'd rather run a mile than discuss anything personal. She had got up to mischief because he supplied no stimulus; all her nonsense was an effort to create a bit of interest. Angela didn't like my mother, but she said she felt sorry for her; born in a different generation, given an education, she could have been a successful entrepreneur or maybe a politician – after all, she certainly had a way with words.

My grandmother had rarely exchanged confidences with me, but once, when there was a coolness between my parents during a visit, she had commented that it reminded her of the time my mother had run away from my father. I was all ears, eager for the gossip but undermined by it too; looking back, my grandmother was playing her own game in telling this to a boy of thirteen. She revealed to me that my mother had abandoned my father in London when she was six months pregnant with Dermot, and turned up without warning at the cottage near Bantry. She had left him, she said, because he wouldn't talk to her; when he came home from work he stuck his nose in a book and there was no budging him. Letters went back and forth across the Irish sea. It struck me that my father hadn't shown himself over-enthusiastic to retrieve his bride; had it not occurred to him to hop on a boat himself or was he already, even in those early days, baffled and paralysed by her moods and actions? My mother gave birth to Dermot and stayed on. My father finally arrived and took her back to

England; his first-born son was four months old before he set
eyes on him.

A nurse stopped and asked if I was okay. I nodded and ran
my hands over my face, settling my expression. As I walked
towards my mother's bed I saw that she was sitting propped
up, a small dish of ice-cream in front of her.

'Hi. How's the ice-cream?'

'Tasteless. What's the matter with ye? Ye look as if ye've
seen a ghost.'

'No, I'm okay, it must be the heat in here.'

'Ye've been talking to the doctor, haven't ye? Have they
had the results? 'Tis bad news, I can tell by yeer face.' She was
alarmed, twitching at the sheet.

'They're worried about your liver, it's in a bad way.'

'Oh.' There was a world of knowledge in her expression.
She pushed dismissively at the dish. 'Take this ould ice-cream
away, would ye? I told the nurse or whatever she is that I
didn't want it, but sure they don't listen. I'm just a number
in a bed.'

I moved the thawing creamy pool to her cabinet. The rosemary I had picked was lying there, a little tired but still faintly
aromatic. I rubbed it between my fingers and held them under
her nose.

'Can you smell it?'

'Just. Lovely.'

'You can smell some fresh tomorrow. There's good news;
you're coming home.'

'I won't be coming back in?'

'No, you can say goodbye to this place.' I flinched, thinking
I sounded crass, but she didn't respond.

'What time am I going? Will ye take me? I don't want an
ambulance.'

'All that's being sorted out. I'll tell them that I'm fetching
you.'

She nodded. 'Did Dermot get away safe?'

'Yes. He rang from the airport.'

91

'He didn't stay long. I thought he might manage more than a stingy couple of days.'

'It's not easy for him to drop everything.'

'Where there's a will there's a way, as they say.' She pulled a face.

'Have you any pain?'

'Not much, just at the base of me spine from lying on this bleddy mattress. 'Tis as hard as nails.'

'You'll be in your own bed tomorrow.'

My father came slowly through into the ward, his joints seized with tiredness. Sitting down, he took her hand.

'I suppose Rory's told you, you're out tomorrow.'

'That's if ye want me. I might be too much trouble to ye.'

He shook his head. 'Ah now, Kitty, don't be saying things like that.'

For once, I knew, she really meant it; it wasn't just said for effect. Her deep fear was that we wouldn't cope or wouldn't want to. Her pale, waxy face looked up at us; her temples had sunk further and strands of her hair decorated the pillow. In that moment I felt the dissolution of years of tension and struggle; I saw that for now, none of it mattered. She was my flesh and blood and until her blood was stilled I would help her raise her banner.

It was arranged that she would be discharged at two the next afternoon. I spent the evening and following morning cleaning the cottage and moving furniture; she was going to be given a zimmer frame to walk with, so I cleared a path to the bathroom. My father phoned Dermot to give him the diagnosis and tell him our plans for her homecoming. We discussed sleeping arrangements and agreed that it would be best if she had the double bed in their bedroom to herself. The room was big enough to accommodate an extra single for him, so I carried one through from the spare room. I called London, explaining to the manager at the health clinic that I would be away for at least another few weeks and checking that my temporary replacement was satisfactory. Another call to a friend ensured that my house-plants would be watered and mail forwarded. I put the phone down and placed my other life on hold.

My father had slept badly again. I persuaded him to let me fetch my mother; he could have the kettle on for our return and keep the fire sweet. I hoped he'd have a nap during my absence. As I drove the weary road to the hospital I tried to banish the thought that this would be the last time she would come home, but it was there, whispering all the way.

She was ready when I got there, sitting in a wheelchair with her handbag in her lap. I fixed one of her woolly hats on; it was sharply cold outside. Two nurses helped us to the car and I tucked a blanket I'd brought around her, swaddling her like a baby.

'Thank God and his blessed mother I'm out of that place,' she said as we left the hospital behind. 'I'm sure I was robbed in there, there was a shifty-looking cleaner and I'd swear she had a fiver off me.'

'I didn't know you'd taken money in.'

'I had me purse, didn't I? Still and all, I don't know why I'm worrying me head over it. I won't be needing money much longer.'

I glanced at her but she turned her head away to look through the side window. She stayed that way for the rest of the journey, gazing out, now and again extricating a hand from beneath the blanket to clear the glass. At the top of the lane she asked me to stop for a minute. The light was fading but the valley was still barely visible, a purple and grey hollow. The car heater hummed softly. She leaned forward slightly, shading her eyes as if there was a bright sun and then told me to drive on.

The hospital had loaned a zimmer frame, a rubber ring to place under her in bed, and a frame to rest pillows on so that she could be propped up.

'Ye Gods,' my father said when he came out to the car,

'you have more equipment with you than the Queen takes to Balmoral.'

'Never mind yeer ould talk,' she said, 'get me inside.'

I carried her in and sat her in her Captain's chair by the fire. She sighed with gratitude at its licking flames and stretched her feet towards it.

'That's grand all together. It's what you miss in them ould hospitals. The heat in there was terrible dry, it made me throat sore.'

We installed the equipment in the bedroom and I placed the zimmer near her chair.

'Ye needn't think I'm using that ould yoke,' she told me, 'I can't get the hang of it at all. I told that ould bossy one in the hospital. I might as well have been talking to the wall.'

'What hang is there to get? You just pick up and lean, pick up and lean.'

She shook her head, pulling a face. 'I might fall, I don't trust it. I'll use me blackthorn stick.'

'You probably will fall if you rely on that, it's not enough.'

'Don't be going on at me,' she said petulantly, 'I've a splitting skull.'

My father stacked the fire higher for her while I made tea. She drank a few sips and then fell into a doze, her feet raised on a little wicker stool made in one of Father Bhattacharya's mission workshops. My father sat by and watched her, pretending to scan the paper.

I prepared dinner, peeling their home-grown Golden Wonders, washing carrots and trying to remember what you did with chicken. In the end I stuck the bird in a roasting dish and put it in the oven. When I first became a vegetarian, in my early twenties, my mother said special novenas for me, convinced that I would slowly starve to death in front of her eyes. She had never encountered a vegetarian and couldn't accept that a body could be kept together without meat. She came to the conclusion that I would suffer a gradual diminution of essential bone marrow because I had no intake of flesh, that eventually all my bone marrow would be used up and I would collapse inwards. She wouldn't brook my explanations that bone marrow couldn't vanish; I think that she was confused by advertisements featuring dogs who needed marrow-bone jelly and applied this principle to all animals, including humans. For several years after I swapped to a vegetarian diet she would make a point, when I visited, of cooking meals involving meat recipes that I had previously enjoyed. Finding that she couldn't tempt me with these, she would describe how she had found a butcher that sold tasty faggots or a delicious new turkey dish they were doing in Sainsbury's. Once she realized that these tactics weren't working, she weighed me down with bags of nuts, fruit cakes bursting with raisins, sultanas, apricots and almonds and packs of dried fruit; a grown man needed to eat more if he was a vegetarian, she warned me, because meat solidified the flesh and gave a body a bit of ballast. I pictured myself with my skeleton folding inwards, floating through the air and presumably colliding with other vegetarians who had suffered a similar loss of gravity.

My mother slept for a couple of hours. She ate a small piece of chicken for dinner and drank half a glass of milk. Afterwards she perked up and suggested a game of cards; what about twenty-fives? My father found a pack, the same dog-eared ones we used to use in Tottenham. My mother had been a terrible cheat at cards, trying to con tricks and getting uppity if she was challenged. Once, she had become so belligerent during a game of whist that my father had swept the cards up and thrown them to the back of the fire, saying that gambling only ever brought trouble. Now, after a couple of hands her concentration lapsed; she was looking into the fire instead of at the cards. She was ready for bed, she agreed. She made her way to the bathroom using her blackthorn stick, wobbling along. My father hovered behind her, hands out. They looked like a pair of sauntering drunks. My heart was in my mouth. I expected to hear a cry and I went outside for a moment to take some gulps of air, telling myself that when you're dying, you're allowed to be bloody-minded and anyway, why should she change the habit of a lifetime? She managed to get back safely to the bedroom. I helped her into bed and gave her her tablets for the night.

'The nurse will be in in the morning to check on you,' I said, 'and the doctor's coming in the afternoon.'

'Am I some kind of curiosity?' she asked. 'Is the whole of the countryside going to come and have a gander? Are ye selling tickets?'

'Stop that now, Kitty,' my father said, carrying in her hot-water bottle, 'that's a load of old nonsense.'

'I haven't heard the priest mentioned at all,' she countered. 'I want to see Father Brady.'

'I'll ring him in the morning,' I promised.

'Do you want your radio on?' my father asked.

'No. Ye could read me something from *Ireland's Own.*'

My father went to fetch his glasses. I bent down to kiss her. 'Look,' I said, 'I put a vase of rosemary by the bed.'

'So ye did. Ye're a good child, when all's said and done.'

'If you need me in the night, just call. I've put the stuck-up lady by the bed.'

It was a brass bell, shaped in the form of an Edwardian lady with a parasol. My mother had bought it from The Foxy Fella and rung it around the house, saying it would come in handy if anyone was ill and needed to call. The lady had her nose in the air, hence her title.

I washed up and gave Dermot a ring to say that she was home. He said that he'd call tomorrow to speak to her. I poked the fire and sat down with a book. I could hear my father reading to her, a story about banshees; he always read in a flat, monotonous tone. It was good for encouraging sleep.

After a while I heard him close the door and go to the bathroom. He came and sat opposite me to roll a cigarette.

'Will we bother to plan for Christmas at all?' he asked me.

'Why not? I think we should keep things as normal as we can.'

'I thought I might give Con and Una a ring. They'd maybe like to see her.'

Con was his brother in Waterford. 'Ask her first, you know what she's like about visitors.'

Unexpected visitors had always panicked her. In Tottenham, she had been known to hide in the cupboard under the stairs in case the person knocking on the door should glance through a window. I had once been unceremoniously bundled behind the sofa when a particularly persistent neighbour, a Mrs Cox, had called. My mother had lain on her stomach beside me, breathing stertorously and crushing me against the wall, her feet sticking out past the end of the furniture. The neighbour had looked through the window, seen her legs and feet, decided that she was dead or unconscious and called an ambulance. My mother, beetroot red, had had to respond to the subsequent urgent knocking and I was told to keep my gob shut while she put on her most baffled look and said that she had been spring cleaning behind the sofa and can't have heard Mrs Cox over the noise of the Hoover. When the frustrated ambulance men had gone, Mrs Cox had been cursed as a nosy jade who'd do better to mind her own bleddy business and stop bothering people in their own homes. She had been struck off the Christmas card list.

'If she needs anything during the night, make sure to call me,' I told my father.

'I'll be up anyway, I always am. You might as well get your sleep and let me have naps in the day.' He re-lit his cigarette and wound a loose thread around a button on his cardigan. He spoke so softly I wondered if he was talking to himself. 'I never thought I'd hear myself say the words, but I hope she goes quickly.'

The Picasso of Tottenham

Maybe Angela was right about my mother; maybe all those years of marshalling her pill bottles, spending days prostrate in an invalid's chair, plotting battle tactics against Assumpta, scouring second-hand shops and stuffing herself to obesity were the activities of a woman who'd never found a productive way of channelling her energies. Perhaps a lot of it was done to attract my father's interest, an effort to get him to express something, anything. Certainly, the books of Angela's that I read in an effort to be a new kind of man suggested as much. The irony for my mother was that she succeeded in driving my father further in on himself; how many times had I seen his guarded, shuttered expression when he walked through the door? He had a habit of rolling his eyes right up under the lids and closing them. When the emotional atmosphere held a particularly high charge, he vanished to the allotment for hours or crawled under his car outside. I identified with him as a boy, aligning myself with his controlled, low-key responses to her. The irony for me was that Angela's books helped me to understand my mother a little better, to allow an adult compassion into my heart, but for reasons I still haven't fathomed they couldn't help my struggling marriage.

During the periods when my mother had one of her part-time jobs, life was less subject to surprises. I was always pleased when she announced that she was making a start in a new 'situation' as she referred to it, even though the down-side was that she would be stashing a new supply of loot to go jaunting with. She had a variety of employments; usually she went for cleaning work – which always struck me as odd given that her own home was a grimy mess and she showed absolutely no interest in tidying it – but she also dabbled in a bakery, a sweet shop and an outsize ladies' clothes store. These jobs would end because she was subject to her nerves again or because some ould one had looked pass remarkable at her or there was a maggoty manager who had no sympathy for a woman with murderous hot flushes.

The lulls between jobs were the times when I kept my head down. There was no knowing what might be going on at home, but it was certain that a new hobby would be enthusiastically introduced. We lived through lace-making, when every chair was treated to a frothy head-rest and our plates and cups had to sit on lace doilies; crocheting, when our jumpers and chair cushions grew peculiar woolly fringes in contrasting colours; candle-making, when all sizes and shapes of candles burned around the rooms, giving the impression that someone was conducting black masses; and – one of the most alarming – poker-work, which involved small round burn marks appearing on many of the wooden items in the house like a rampant outbreak of measles.

I would travel back on the school bus sunk in gloom and with a sense of trepidation. I eyed my friends chatting around me; none of them were returning to an eccentric woman with a penchant for sudden and strange interests. My two closest friends had mothers who did part-time secretarial jobs, attended the Women's Institute, sang in church choirs and made jam or chutney in season; how wonderful that was, how acceptable and intensely comforting. How I envied them.

I might turn my key in the door, for example, and sniff a powerful aroma of paint and varnish. She would be ensconced at the living-room table. The unwashed breakfast dishes would have been swept to one side and the rest of the surface covered in plastic flowerpots and piles of shells. In her overwhelming enthusiasm for her new hobby, she would have forgotten to take her hat and coat off. Then the story would spill out; she had been looking through the window of a craft shop in Forest Gate and seen a *gorgeous* display of shell-covered pots and boxes. The shop owner had sat down with her and gone through a book called *Hundreds of Ways with Shells* which illustrated all the fascinating uses these simple objects could be put to. They could be varnished, painted, stained, polished or left *au naturel* and glued to – well, to anything, basically.

She had bought six large bags of shells, a box of oil paints, a bottle of varnish, a tub of glue and a dozen pots to start her off so that she could get the hang of it. She'd be like Picasso yet, she assured me, straightening her hat and reading the directions on the glue. That was my cue to sink down despairingly and watch her busying away at a pot. Shells were daubed in bright colours, left to dry, glued and randomly attached to the plastic surfaces. I heard a documentary commentator's voice in my head, circa the year 3,500: 'these examples of primitive art were unearthed in the London area which was known as Tottenham. They demonstrate an interesting naïveté and were obviously done by an untrained hand, but what they lack in artistic merit is perhaps compensated for by the sheer enthusiasm they express.' There had been a bronze and an iron age, I thought; why not a shell age?

The pots would only be a starting point. Soon, vibrantly-coloured shells started to appear throughout the house, as if they were breeding. The bathroom mirror frame was edged with them, a line of them snaked around the mantelpiece and along the front of the fire-guard, they coated the kitchen window-ledge and climbed the stairs along the edge of the banister. They erupted into the garden, hugging tubs of gladioli and attaching themselves to the water butt.

Decorated pots and mugs were produced for the church raffle. To my horror, I picked up my lunch-box one morning and found that red, green and orange shells formed my initials on the lid. It took me half an hour to prise them off with a chisel and residual glue stuck to my fingers for days. After a few weeks the hobby palled. As a last fling, she tried brightening up a dress with shells, attaching them to the hem, neckline and wrists, but the glue wasn't effective. My father found a yellow shell in his soup and she was shedding them as she walked; they made a crunching sound, like a snail under foot.

Wine-making was her passion one year. She had read in the *Universe*, a Catholic paper, that some parish priests were finding it hard to make ends meet and were having to water down the altar wine. This shocked her; after all, the wine turned into the blood of Christ during transubstantiation and therefore watered wine meant that Christ's blood was being tampered with. It was true that Jesus had turned water into wine, but that was a different class of thing entirely because he had the power to perform miracles and being the son of God, was entitled to act as he liked. Those priests might be dicing with the salvation of their souls she decided and she headed off to discuss the intricacies of this theological issue with Father Corcoran. The good Father, who spent most of his days in a stout-induced haze and had a tenuous grasp on reality, humoured her and said that yes, he was sure that if she wanted to make fine strong wine he'd be able to get it to some of those poor priests who were skating on thin ice.

A woman fired with a purpose, she came home and wrote to the *Universe* telling them of her plan and suggesting that other Catholics might like to do the same. It struck her that priests working in missions in poverty-stricken areas of Africa and other such far-flung places might have a similar problem, so she despatched a letter to Father Bhattacharya, asking would she need an export licence to send wine through the post? I was sent to the library to fetch a book on wine-making. Equipment was bought in bulk; a dozen demijohns, six fermentation bins, air-locks, bungs and siphon tubes. My father was given orders to pick elderberries and blackberries and instructed to excavate buckets of potatoes from the allotment. The greengrocer delivered a sack of parsnips.

The house was filled with the heady tang of fruit, yeast and sugar. For days it was hard to scavenge food because the tiny kitchen had been taken over by vegetable peelings and containers of diced potatoes and parsnips. My mother's hands turned purple. Bins full of first-stage ingredients sat in the hallway, living-room and bathroom, burping quietly. She had inserted one under the dining table on which I regularly barked my shins. During pauses in conversation the fermentation could be heard; *gloop gloop*. The smells percolated throughout the house; even my clothes seemed to exude a boozy fragrance and I felt muddle-headed.

I think that maybe, true to Angela's belief, my mother was a scientist *manqué*. Significantly, she wore a white apron when she was brewing. The demijohns, the siphons, the sight of fermentation, filled her with delight. She was imbued with a belief that her task encompassed a miraculous transformation. She loved playing with the tubes, counting campden tablets and sorting out air locks. I would come upon her sitting at the table with a demijohn in front of her, just watching the process taking place. Isn't it incredible, she'd say, that a humble parsnip or elderberry could be turned into a liquid that would itself turn into Christ's blood? Sure, didn't God move in mysterious ways and didn't he have his eyes on every lowly thing on this earth?

The elderberry and parsnip wines proved a success and were bottled; boxes full were delivered to Father Corcoran at the presbytery. I have no idea whether any of them found their way to the needy priests. Father Corcoran had to be accompanied home on several occasions afterwards, when he had turned up at a whist drive or meeting of the Saint Vincent de Paul Society in a tired and emotional state. He vanished for a couple of months later that year and was reported to be convalescing in the country after a debilitating bout of gastric flu.

The potato wine was a different and explosive story. My mother had stored it out of sight in the cupboard under the stairs. Little was said about this particular batch, but there had been problems with the fermentation process and she had been seen poring over that section in the library book. She was grumpy about her lack of success because coming from the land of poitín, she thought she should have a natural born talent for encouraging the alcohol out of spuds. Maybe, my father had suggested, the potatoes had been the wrong variety but she pooh-poohed him, saying any old murphy should do the business.

I was hopeful that this phase seemed to be drawing to an end. Father Bhattacharya had replied, saying that her generosity was boundless but the native people in the missions liked to make the mass wine and there was no shortage of that particular item. The *Universe* failed to print her letter, so her idea was lost to the wider Catholic public. None of us in the house drank wine, so it was unlikely that she'd make more. My father and I were glad that we could find the kettle again and that decent dinners were back on the agenda.

One evening, as we were eating, the potato wine erupted with the force of a small nuclear explosion in the cupboard. An ocean of cloudy liquid started to leak into the hallway. It took the three of us a long time to clear the cupboard out and wash the hall carpet. Despite our efforts, the lower floor of the house smelled like an alcoholic's lair for months. My father made the mistake of saying that it was a pity to see a waste of good spuds; they'd have made fine shepherd's pies or mash. My mother retorted that it was easy enough to stand back and sneer; Our Lord himself had been sneered at in his time and she'd only been trying to work for the glory of God.

SEVEN

The day after my mother's return from hospital was busy, with the nurse and doctor in attendance. Her morphine dosage was checked; she didn't appear to have much pain and she lay quietly, letting them move swiftly around her.

The doctor accepted a cup of tea when he'd finished, following me into the kitchen.

'I suppose,' he said, 'this kind of thing isn't new to you. You're a physiotherapist, aren't you?'

'That's right. I spent a bit of time on an oncology ward when I was training. I know roughly what to expect.'

'No,' Molloy corrected me. 'You don't know what to expect; she's your mother and that makes it completely different.'

'I knew she was dying as soon as I saw her,' I pointed out.

He sipped his tea. 'If only she'd kept her appointments or let me in when I came to see her. Don't get me wrong, I honestly don't think I could have done anything that would have affected the course of events, but there's always that element of doubt.'

When he'd gone I went out to clear leaves from the gutters, raking at them fiercely. I rammed them into a bin-bag, wishing that he'd kept his mouth shut. I was angry with her for playing games just when she shouldn't have. All those years of trotting to the doctor's when there was very little wrong and then keeping him at bay when there was every reason to see him.

I worked up a sweat, going on to rake up all the leaves in the garden, picking up twigs and other debris.

I cleaned out the bird bath I'd bought for her a few birthdays ago. She'd scratched on the stone base in black biro, in the way she wrote on anything she was given: 'To his mother on her 72nd birthday from her loving son Rory, May 1993, xxxx.' I traced the words with my finger; I'd always laughed in amusement at this foible. Now I conjectured about why she'd done it. Were those the sentiments she longed for me to write? She liked fulsome words of affection, big gestures, the kind I shrank from making. She chose the type of greetings cards that I rejected in the shops, those in pastel colours featuring kittens or huge bunches of flowers with sentimental verses inside. I received one of those from her every year, with TO MY SON on the front in gold-edged letters. Inside, she would score a line under the words in the verse that she wished to emphasize, with a double line wherever it mentioned LOVE. I sent her cards featuring reproductions of great artists, blank inside except for my own simple greeting, knowing as I licked the envelopes that she would prefer gaudy, eye-catching efforts describing perfect motherhood. The rhyme on the sewing kit Dermot had once bought her was the kind that sent her into transports:

> Mother sweet and gentle,
> Thoughtful, kind and true,
> Giving love unending,
> Mother, that is you.

Her favourite songs were syrupy ballads featuring mothers; 'Silver-haired Mother of Mine', 'A Mother's Love's a Blessing', and best of all 'Mother Machree' as sung by Count John McCormack. She and Father Corcoran often crooned it together during an evening chin-wag, he with a bottle in his hand and cake plate balanced on his knee, she with her tea poured specially for the occasion into a bone china cup:

105

Oh, I love the dear silver that shines in your hair
And the brow that's all furrowed and wrinkled with care
Oh, I kiss the dear fingers so tire-worn for me
Oh, God bless you and keep you, Mother Machree.

Now, as I hung the bird bath back up I considered how mean
I had been not to write this simple kind of message that would
have meant so much to her. Yet, at the same time, I thought
how like her it was to shape something the way she wished it
to be, to mould it to her will.

That evening, as I was sorting her pillows out at bed-time,
she beckoned me close.

'Is yeer father out of the way?'

'He's having a bath, why?'

'Go over to the bottom drawer below the wardrobe. There's
a brown box. Bring it here to me.'

I did as she asked, laying the long box beside her on the
bed. She touched the lid of it, patting gently. Then she asked
me to open it. Inside, beneath several layers of white tissue
paper, was a dark brown robe with a hood and buttons down
the front. I lifted it up, thinking that it was the kind of vestment
I might have worn if I'd become a monk.

'That's me shroud,' she said. 'I sent away to Dublin for it.
That's what I want on me. I want to be dressed in that with
the hood pulled up. D'ye understand?'

I nodded, the cloth cold and soft under my hand. A musty
air like a draught in a tomb rose from it.

'Me mother had one the same. She looked lovely in it, like
a princess. Put it away now, I don't want yeer father seeing
it. 'Twould only upset him. He's not strong at all.'

'How long have you had this?' I asked, for something to
say.

'Three years. They were advertised in the paper.'

I settled the box back in its drawer. I couldn't help wondering if there was any other country in the world where you'd
be able to get a shroud by mail-order. I was trying to distract

myself from the thought of her in it; it had looked huge and she was shrinking daily. Even her distended stomach had reduced in size.

'What date is it?' she asked.

'November twenty-second.'

'I want ye to buy me some Christmas cards tomorrow,' she said. 'I'll need to get them sent off. There's a place in Fermoy that does them. Nice religious ones, now, none of yeer ould doves or bells, yokes like that. Pictures of the nativity or the wise men. And make sure they have a . . .'

'. . . Nice verse inside,' I finished.

'Oh very funny, ha ha.'

I moved around, folding clothes and emptying the ashtray by my father's bed. His nocturnal smoking had been a bone of contention between them for years. She alleged that one day he'd burn them alive and there would be no funeral expenses, with only ashes left. He would reply that we all had to go sometime and the man upstairs would decide when; if it said 'frying tonight' on their ticket then that's the way it would be.

When I turned around to ask her if she wanted to be read to she was asleep, her lips open slightly. A little of the plain yoghurt she'd eaten for supper had curdled in the corner of her mouth. I took a tissue, damped it on my tongue and dabbed the food away. She gave a soft snore. I wondered if she would dream and if the illness destroying her body would rise up and invade her dreams also, turning them dark and fearful. I had picked fresh rosemary again that morning, replenishing her vase. I took a sprig and laid it on her pillow so that the fragrance might inspire dreams of a far off fantastic land of spices and heat and palaces with musical fountains.

The next day she was restless, becoming agitated about Father Brady, the parish priest, who had arranged to call at two o'clock. She spent the whole morning giving us instructions about the little altar she wanted set up in the bedroom. There was scarcely enough room between the two beds, but

I had to carry in a small oak table from the kitchen. My father
ironed a white tablecloth and she watched him through the
door, telling him to make sure every single crease was gone.
Once the cloth had been fitted and the corners smoothed I
had to place her six-inch high crucifix in the middle of the
table. Statues of Our Lady and The Sacred Heart were positioned diagonally at either end, facing in to the crucifix.

'D'you want flowers on it?' my father asked her.

'What flowers? There's none in the garden this time of the
year.'

'Rory could get some in Fermoy, couldn't you, son?'

'Yes, I could pop in now; I've got to go for your Christmas
cards anyway.'

'No, leave it,' she said. 'I want you to be here for the priest,
you can go shopping when he's been.'

I couldn't help looking at her with some suspicion. She was
lying half-propped up, her face nearly as pale as the pillow.
There was no reason why I should stay for the priest; I had
abandoned Catholicism over twenty years ago and told my
parents at the time. Every now and again my mother would
raise the issue of my lost faith and I would divert the conversation, unwilling to hear her pious sentiments. Sometimes,
when I unpacked at home after a visit to them I would find a
pamphlet hidden amongst my clothes: *Returning to the Faith*
or *Questions Lapsed Catholics Ask*. Once, a copy of a prayer
entitled *For Those Who Have Lost Their Way* fell out of my
washbag as I fumbled for my razor; she had underlined the
part where it said that it was never too late to come back to
the church; '<u>God in his goodness loves even the most heinous
of sinners.</u>' It was a long time since I'd seen that word, *heinous*;
it made me think of serial killers, dictators who ordered geno-
cide. What on earth did she suspect me of? Booklets arrived
a couple of times a year from The Catholic Way organization;
then I knew that she had been filling coupons in in my name,
a response to adverts that appeared in the press; *Have You
Been Wondering About the Meaning of Your Life?* and *Ever*

Thought of Talking to Jesus? These attempts to persuade me with holy literature were never mentioned between us; it felt like aerial bombardment, a counter-offensive devised at Heavenly HQ.

I have many memories of priests' visits to the house in my childhood; often I would be commandeered to recite a prayer or sing a song. My mother would hiss at me to go and put on a clean shirt and I would be positioned by the window to do my turn. I felt like a tortoise tormented from its shell. I was not one of those children who like to show off their dramatic talents; I was shy, desperate to go unnoticed. Squirming, I would half-close my eyes to put the smiling, nodding priest out of focus while I performed. Father Corcoran always asked for 'Kitty of Coleraine' and when I'd finished he would lean over me, breathing stout into my face and saying I had the voice of an angel.

I had never met Father Brady, only glimpsed him at a distance when I'd occasionally given my mother a lift to mass because my father wasn't well. I had no doubt that he would have been told all about me; my loss of faith, my failed marriage, perhaps even my strange abandonment of real food. My mother would have entreated his prayers for me and requested masses to be offered up in the hope that I would return to the bosom of the church. I steeled myself for his arrival as I decanted liquid from her plastic bottle of Lourdes water into a glass bowl and placed it on the home altar; she wanted the priest to bless her with this special ingredient. I felt awkward and ham-fisted arranging these religious items; they meant nothing to me. She could have got my father to deal with them, but I was sure that she had involved me deliberately, seizing any opportunity to influence my sinner's soul.

Brady breezed in on the dot of two. He was a small, beefy man with plump hands, a fast talker from Kerry. My father took him in to my mother and I kept out of the way in the kitchen, occupying myself with making a soup. I sensed that old rigid fear of being trapped; I almost believed that any minute now, my mother might call me and ask me to say that nice poem about the daffodils for Father Brady. I could hear him in the bedroom, rattling through prayers, barely giving my mother time to make responses. He was finished in ten minutes and out of the house by two twenty. I felt cheated on her behalf; surely your spiritual adviser should spend a bit longer than that with you when you are dying. She had been so anxious about his coming and yet a mere neighbour would have stayed longer and indulged in a bit of social chat.

My father was sitting on the side of the bed, lighting a candle for her.

'He didn't overstay his welcome,' I said.

'He's a busy man,' my mother replied, but I thought she sounded flat. She was lying back, all the morning's energy gone.

'He'll be back again, sure,' my father said. 'We'll carry the altar out as it is so that it's ready another time.'

I popped back in to see her before I left for Fermoy.

'You look exhausted, try to have a sleep,' I said.

She looked at me and her eyes seemed opaque. 'Me mother was a good woman, she helped lots of people,' she murmured.

'I'm sure she did.'

'A good woman and a good mother. She always did her best for us and them were hard times.'

'They were, Mum, very hard.'

It was only three o'clock, but dusk was creeping up to the window. The candle's yellow light emphasized her waxy complexion and the shadows under her eyes.

'There's a noise of an aeroplane in here,' she said more urgently. 'Is there a fella flying about?'

I swallowed. 'No, no aeroplanes in here. You're okay, it must be something you're imagining. The medicine can do that to you.'

She rubbed her lips with the sheet. 'Me skin's terrible dry.'

'Here.' I applied some of her lip-cream. She pursed her lips up for me, making me smile.

110

'Yeer hair needs a cut,' she told me. 'Ye have good hair, like me.'

'Maybe I'll get a chance to have it done in Fermoy.'

'Don't forget; nice cards.'

'I won't.'

'Did ye speak to Father Brady at all?'

'Not really, just hallo.'

'I suppose, Rory, ye might come back to the faith one day. I pray to God every night of me life that ye will.'

I clenched my jaw, then relaxed. I stood and smoothed her sheet, looking down on my helpless tormentor.

'Maybe, Mum. You never know what'll happen, do you? Now have a sleep and if you're up to it we'll write your cards this evening.'

Fermoy was busy and rain-swept. I looked at Christmas lights and decorations and gave a pound to a Santa who shook a collection tin at me. I knew that Christmas was approaching, the signs were all around me, but I felt distant from it. It was going to have to happen and I thought that we should make an effort to observe it, but I felt no involvement. I wandered through shops, buying food, wondering what I could tempt my mother with. She was eating very little. I decided on a raspberry sorbet and a pack of lemon ice-lollies; her mouth was constantly dry. In the chemist's I noticed a pack of 4711 cologne wet-wipes and bought them. It was the only scent she had ever worn; it brought back train and coach and boat journeys. I sniffed at the box as I handed the money over. Maybe, I thought, I would put some in the coffin with her, tucked into her shroud. In the card shop I bought several packs; scenes of the adoration of the Magi, shepherds watching flocks, a Madonna and baby. I checked that they all contained rhyming Christmas wishes. Several people stopped me in the street, people I recognized vaguely, and asked me how my mother was. I thanked them for their good wishes, remembering to check their names so that I could tell her. I found that this interest from strangers pierced me, bringing tears to my eyes. I had my hair cut in a barber's, day-dreaming as he trimmed. I saw my mother in her bed, her rosary clasped by her ear. Part of me was back there, in the cottage. I knew that until she died I wouldn't feel at home in my own body. I had an urgent wish to get back and startled the barber by twitching in the chair and asking him to finish quickly.

That night she came out into the living-room for a while and ate a couple of spoons of sorbet. Then we formed a Christmas card production line; she dictated what she wanted me to write and when I'd finished I handed the card to my father who addressed and stamped the envelope. Although she'd been keen to do the cards, she seemed half-hearted and distracted again. I had to keep prompting her and my father gazed at her anxiously.

'Are you all right, Kitty? Do you want to stop?'

'No, no. Carry on there. We need to get the job done.'

I understood, I thought, that she was setting herself little tasks. There were formalities to be observed: the priest, the cards, the visit from my father's family, calls from neighbours. When, I wondered, might she decide that they were completed and would that be the moment when she'd go?

There was one subject I'd been loath to bring up, but this seemed the right time. I'd mentioned it to my father, but I could tell from his daunted expression that he couldn't tackle it.

'Mum, do you want any of your family contacted? I could do that if you like.'

She chewed at her lip and pulled her blanket around her. My father tidied the stack of cards, squaring them.

'Ye could write to Biddy, if she's still there. Maybe she's dead. They might all be dead and buried for all I know.' She shivered. 'I'm cold, this ould room's awful draughty.'

My father rattled the fire and stacked turf on. She had always loved a big fire with a red-hot glow. In Tottenham she would build chimney roarers, defying the law and continuing to use ordinary coal instead of smokeless because she said it gave out better heat. One evening, when my father was on a late shift, she had set the chimney ablaze and had had to call the fire brigade. The head fireman had gazed at her in awe and asked her what had she been trying to do, roast an ox? She had muttered to his departing back that he was so sharp he'd better watch out or he might cut himself. Then she had set about clearing away all signs of the disaster, saying that I wasn't to mention it to my father; he'd be tired out when he got in and it wasn't worth worrying him. I knew that this was nonsense and that the reason she didn't want him to know was because he'd warned her many times about her enthusiastic fires, predicting just such an event.

Dermot rang, as he did every night, speaking first to me or my father, then to my mother. Afterwards, as she made her tortuous way to the bathroom, leaning on her stick, she spoke to herself: 'Ah sure, we didn't do so bad with our children, not so bad at all.'

A Test from God

A point would come, during each summer holiday near Bantry, when my mother and grandmother had a falling out. A coolness would set in for a couple of days. This falling out was sometimes over an incident, such as the time when my mother let the pig into the vegetable garden and it decimated the cabbages, but more often than not there was no apparent cause. I would know that the falling out was signalled when my grandmother headed off up the fields to see her neighbours, the Donavans. Then my mother would take me on a trip to Cork.

We would rise early and walk the three miles to Bantry to wait for the bus or the bone-shaker, as my mother called it. It was a low-slung vehicle with a long-lost suspension, driven by a distant cousin of hers, Denny Sullivan. Denny had thick pebble glasses, a fat upper lip and a permanently lop-sided grin. He wore wellingtons all year round.

My grandmother had told me that Denny was a bit gone in the head, that one of the fairies had sneaked into his cot when he was a baby and stolen some of his sense for the fairy king. Now and again, about three times a year, Denny would have one of his 'episodes' and take off with the bus. Ignoring his waiting passengers he accelerated past them and headed for Athlone. Apparently he liked the safe feeling of being in the very middle of Ireland. The police in Athlone knew him, and would ring the bus company in Bantry to tell them he was back. He would park overnight in the main street, buy himself chips, chocolate and Little Nora lemonade and sleep in the bus after feasting royally. The next day he drove home and carried on as normal, comforted by his trip to Ireland's womb.

114

Although Denny spoke extremely slowly I found his rolling accent almost impenetrable, but my mother would chat away to him as he lazed his way to Cork at twenty miles an hour. He was fascinated by all things English and would ask her about London.

'Tell me now, have ye been to see de Towerrr and Buckingham Palis?'

'Oh, ages ago. The Queen was there when we went to the palace.'

'Did ye see herrr?'

'No, no. But the flag was up.'

'And do ye have dem moving shtairrs, dem tings?'

'Escalators. Oh, we do. We have loads of them in the Underground.'

'And what's dat?'

'There's trains that go under the ground all around London.'

'Yerra Jaysus God! Arrre ye takin' de mickey?'

'Not at all. Sure it's been there years.'

'And tell me now, do ye have dem colourrred people in London, de ones wit de darrrk shkins?'

'There's people from India living a few doors away, sure.'

'And would dere be an odourrr frrrom deirrr shkins now?'

'I don't think so.'

'Well now, tell me; do ye tink 'tis betterrr to live in London or New Yorrrk?'

That would have her flummoxed. 'Well sure, I couldn't be saying that because I haven't been to New York.'

'New Yorrrk is verrry big altogetherrr,' Denny would remark sagely and my mother would nod, unable to argue with that.

He must have been terribly fired up by his conversation with her one year because to her horror, he turned up on the doorstep in Tottenham on a fine September morning, the sun glinting off his jam jar specs. He was still wearing his wellingtons. He had broken the habit of fifteen years and driven the bus to Ringaskiddy, where he had caught the ferry to Swansea.

115

He announced that he wanted to get a job on de big rrred London buses and drrrive past de Towerrr and de Palis. In de meantime, did my mother have any Little Norrra limonade as he was terrrible parrrched and dey'd had divil a dhrop on de trrrain.

My mother took some extra tranquillizers and phoned the priest and my father at work. After a long talk with Denny, Father Corcoran managed to persuade him that London would be an awful place to live; if people here tried to drive buses wherever they liked they got arrested and – this proved to be the clincher – Little Nora lemonade was nowhere to be found in the length and breadth of England. Denny went back quite happily two days later, but it took my mother several months to get over the shock. She was circumspect in her conversations with him after that, taking care not to make London sound attractive.

During the summer of my twelfth year my mother and grandmother had words about who'd had the last of the bacon for breakfast on one Tuesday morning. My mother and I were therefore on Denny's bus by ten, headed for Cork. My mother had noticed in the *Cork Examiner* that a new shop selling religious goods had opened by the quays; Martha and Mary it was called and there were special half-price opening offers. Denny had driven even more slowly than usual because of a suspect axle and we were thirsty when we arrived. My mother decided that we'd have a snack in Maggie Murphy's, one of her preferred watering holes, before we started shopping.

Unfortunately, Maggie Murphy's had changed hands, although it cunningly continued with the same name. The café was up a stairs above a bakery, and the first sign that all was not well was when my mother saw that the usual pristine white linen tablecloths had been replaced with stained red-checked gingham. We gave our order for cheese sandwiches and a pot of tea to a listless young girl.

'Sorry,' she said, not sounding at all sorry, 'we've no cheese.'

'How d'ye mean?' my mother asked.

'We're out of cheese.'

'How can ye be out of cheese? There's a shop that sells it over the road.'

'We don't get it from there, we have it delivered and it hasn't come.'

The girl tossed her long hair back and I saw my mother stiffen.

'I've been coming here for ten years and I've never known ye to run out of cheese.'

'I'll have egg,' I volunteered, wanting to deflect an argument.

My mother shot me a look. 'Could ye not go and get cheese from over the road just this once? I've a hankering for cheese.'

'No,' said the girl simply.

My mother's bosom juddered. 'I see. That's the way of things, is it? I'll just have tea, so, and bring egg for me son.'

The girl scribbled disinterestedly on her pad and left us.

'Oh, hold on!' My mother winked at me and gestured.

The girl stopped in her tracks, sighed, blinked and sloped back.

'Have ye a scone?'

'Yes.'

'I'll have two of them with jam. I suppose ye have jam?'

'Yes.'

My mother picked up the tablecloth after she'd gone and fingered the wood underneath. 'Dirty,' she said with satisfaction. 'This ould place has gone downhill. Look at the sugar bowl, there's crusty bits at the edges. I wouldn't be surprised if they bring the milk bottle to the table.'

There were crusty bits around the sugar bowl at home but I forbore to mention this. I looked at the prints of the Blasket Islands on the walls.

'I stopped her gallop though,' my mother commented *sotto voce*. 'Did you see the way I called her back? Barefaced young jade.'

After a long quarter of an hour during which my mother drummed her fingers on the table and pronounced that if this was the way Ireland was going, Dev might as well not have bothered arguing with John Bull, the girl slouched in with a tray.

'Did ye have to go to India for the tea?' my mother asked.

The girl didn't answer, but shoved our food onto the table and left a bill by the milk. Her feet slip-slopped from her shoes as she vanished.

'Look at the cut of her,' my mother said, attacking a scone. ' 'Twould be a long day before you'd get a civil answer out of that one.'

'Maybe her dog's just died,' I said.

My mother pulled a face as she bit into her scone. 'This ould thing's stale, I'd say they've had it a week. What's the sandwich like?'

'All right.'

'Hmm. Let's try the tea. That's always been good here, strong enough to cut with a knife.'

It was thin and pale, a poor imitation of the brew she'd been anticipating.

'Ye wouldn't credit it, would ye?' my mother asked. ' 'Tis like ould donkey's wee-wee. That one did it on purpose. I could tell she was going to do the dirty.' She picked up the bill. 'The cheek of it! A pound for ould rubbish that wouldn't satisfy a starving man and it was the last thing on this earth to eat! Finish up there, will ye, I want to get out of this hellhole.'

I gamely swallowed my dry sandwich, washing it down with gulps of the donkey's wee-wee. As I finished, my mother grabbed the teapot and up-ended it, creating a lake on the table and floor. Then she took a spoon and scooped strawberry jam into the flood, smearing it in well. It looked like modern art, the kind of effort where the artist flings paint randomly at the canvas.

'That'll show them,' she said, hoisting her bag.

The sullen girl appeared as she threw the money onto the sodden, jammy table.

'Dreadfully sorry,' my mother said in her pseudo upper-class accent, 'we had a little accident, don'tcha kneow. I'm afraid yew've got some work to do, I hope yew don't pass out with the shock.'

Martha and Mary improved my mother's mood. She became positively gleeful when we stepped through the door. The counters and shelves were chock full of items to aid devotion, made by the needy and deserving; a heady combination. There were piles of framed holy pictures produced in a workshop for the blind, rosaries from an African cooperative, crucifixes in all sizes and three types of wood from a leper colony, prayer books sent from the Punjab, mass cards from secret Catholic groups in Poland, musical plastic holy water fonts made by polio victims and hymnals illustrated by paralysed artists who painted with their brushes in their mouths. She bought a picture of the holy family featuring a very plump baby Jesus, a holy water font that played 'Silent Night' when you dipped a finger in and a bottle of holy water blessed by the Bishop of Cork to go with it.

We sat down on a sun-warmed bench by the River Lee so that she could look again at her purchases. I had to hold the font while she poured some holy water in and tested it. The tinkling strains of the carol rang unseasonally forth.

'That's dotey,' a wistful little voice said.

We looked around. A small girl with ginger hair tied in plaits, wearing a grubby blue-and-white dress with a sailor collar was standing by us.

'D'ye like it?' my mother asked, holding it near her.

'Oh I do, I do,' the little girl said. She had green eyes with brown flecks in them and a solemn expression. She peered more closely. 'Is that Our Lady at the top there?' she asked.

'It is, God's blessed mother.'

The girl pressed her hands together. 'Isn't she beeootiful,' she said. 'I never knew she was so beeootiful.'

'Would ye like to take some holy water?' my mother offered. ''Twill play the tune for ye.'

119

'Can I? Can I really?' She held out a hesitant finger.

'Wisha ye can, of course, alannah. Isn't it lovely to see a child wanting to offer praise to Our Lady? Won't it warm the Virgin's heart?'

My mother's accent was becoming more pronounced. I looked at her curiously.

The girl carefully dipped a tiny finger into the font. 'Silent Night' played for her. Her hands flew dramatically to her cheeks. 'Oh!' she exclaimed, '' tis magic! Is it Our Lady doing that?'

My mother smiled indulgently. 'Well now, maybe 'tis. Who can be the judge? What's yeer name, acushla?'

'Erin.'

'Well, God save the heroes! Isn't that lovely! The very name of Ireland itself! And where's yeer mammy and daddy?'

Erin glanced down. 'Me mammy's dead. Me daddy's gone to sell a horse. He'll be back here for me at six o'clock.'

'He's left ye alone? How old are ye?'

'I'm eight.' She sat down beside my mother who shifted me along to make room. 'Me daddy has to sell the horse, he's done it before. Then he has to have a pint to set him up.' She tapped my mother's arm. 'D'ye see that hotel across the road?'

'I do, what of it?'

Erin laughed. 'I went in there just now and had a bath, 'twas gorgeous. Lashings of hot water and big soft towels. I hardly ever get a bath on the road.'

'Ye little divil ye,' my mother laughed admiringly. 'Are ye travellers then?'

'We are. We travel all over the country.'

'And good for ye!' my mother approved. 'Aren't ye a great little character? And ye're all alone 'til this evening?'

Erin nodded. 'I get a biteen lonely sometimes.'

'Are ye hungry?'

'Starved. I've only had an apple today.' Erin looked up at her. 'Me daddy has no money 'til he sells the horse.'

120

'Ye poor creature ye! Come and have a bite of lunch with me and me son. Rory, say hallo to the little girl.'

I nodded to Erin. I was stunned; in London I'd always been instructed never to go with strangers and here was my mother kidnapping a child. I nudged her.

'What if the police stop us?' I said.

'What? Why would they do that?'

'They might think we're trying to take her away. Her father might be looking for her.'

'Sure didn't ye hear her say her daddy's not coming back 'til six. This isn't England, thank God, a poor child can trust people here. Poor motherless creature.' She patted Erin's hair. Erin smiled and I knew that my mother was putty in her hands. 'Haven't ye gorgeous hair,' my mother told her, 'real true red, not that ould carrotty colour some eejits get out of bottles.'

We set off to have lunch. Erin slipped her arm through my mother's and I trailed after them, looking at the girl's torn dress hem, bare legs and grimy sandals. I couldn't understand this turn of events; my mother had always said to be wary of tinker children, they could be rough.

Erin ate her plate of fish and chips and asked for more. She devoured two large helpings of trifle and three glasses of milk. My mother watched her eating with relish.

'Ye've a great appetite, I love to see a good appetite in a child. This fella here only picks at his food.'

Erin smiled at me. 'Ye talk funny,' she said to me, 'not like yeer mammy at all.'

'That's because he was born in London, pet. He's a little cockney sparrow. Where were ye born?'

'In Tralee. That's where me mammy died.'

'Did ye never know her?'

'No. She went to heaven when I was two weeks old.'

'Ah, ye poor peteen.' My mother's eyes were glistening. 'And yeer daddy's raised ye?'

'One of me aunties helps sometimes but I don't like her, she's horrible.'

'How so?'

'She never gives me enough to eat. Me belly rumbles at night.'

My mother gazed at Erin. 'Oh, I know what that's like, dotey, I know only too well. Have a bit of ice-cream now, do.'

While Erin went to the toilet, my mother settled the bill and shook her head.

'That poor little girl,' she said to me, 'alone in the world with no mother.'

'She's got a father, she's not alone,' I said, churlishly.

'Ah, that's not the same thing at all. Ye wouldn't understand. A girl needs a mother's love. Ye can tell she's missing it, she had the look of a lost child. What kind of father is he anyway, letting an infant that age roam the streets with no food? What if it poured with rain? Them travellers treat their children rough, they have to fend for themselves.' She smiled. 'Did ye hear her, having a bath in that hotel! Isn't she a gutsy little article! Ah, wouldn't I love to tuck her under me arm and carry her home with me!'

I was alarmed; she had an inspired look. I knew that she was capable of sudden, impulsive actions. I pictured Erin back at my grandmother's, running up and down the glen with her pigtails flying, and then in Tottenham, flicking those green eyes at my father. He'd known my mother to come home with some unexpected acquisitions, but never an eight-year-old child.

Erin spent the rest of the day with us, as if we had been on her agenda all along. We went to a department store and bought her a pink and blue dress, matching cardigan and socks, shiny black shoes and white underwear. She allowed my mother to choose the clothes, nodding eagerly at whatever was suggested, then went off with her to the Ladies to put them on. She emerged holding my mother's hand, her hair brushed out and held back with a blue ribbon they'd got at the 'buttons and bows' counter. My mother turned her around in front of a mirror.

'Now,' she said to me, 'what d'ye think?'

'Very nice.' No second-hand shops for Erin, I was thinking dourly.

She nudged Erin. 'Will ye listen to him! "Very nice". What would ye do with boys! D'ye know that rhyme, pet; "What are little girls made of? Sugar and spice and all things nice! What are little boys made of? Rats and snails and puppy dogs' tails!" Have ye never heard it?'

Erin was chuckling. 'No, I never did. 'Tis funny! Rats and snails and puppy dogs' tails!'

'I'm not a little boy, I'm eleven,' I told her.

She pulled a face and moved in closer to my mother.

'Don't mind him, he's just an ould grump,' my mother told her. 'Now, what'll we do?'

'Can we go to the pictures?' Erin asked. 'I've never been to the pictures in me life!'

'We will so. Let's see what's on.'

I always had to argue mercilessly to get my mother to take me to see anything other than a biblical epic. She had once had a bad experience during *Robin Hood* when a boy behind us blew a loud blast on a whistle every time the Sheriff of Nottingham got a trouncing. But today anything seemed possible; off we hurried and got in to *Greyfriars Bobby*, a film I'd already seen with a friend in London. Erin sat on the edge of her seat, mouth open, transfixed. Whenever I looked at my mother she was watching Erin's face or pressing more sweets on her.

We had to get Denny's return bus at five. At half-four we left Erin back where she'd found us.

'I had a grand time,' she said, buttoning her cardigan. 'The best time ever.'

'Did ye, pet? Will ye always remember me?'

'I will.'

'Just tell yeer daddy ye met a kind lady who was yeer mammy for an afternoon.'

'He'll like me dress, I know he will.'

'Don't forget to say a prayer for me at night.'

'I'll say one every night, so I will, for ever.'

Erin waved at us until we turned the corner, her cardigan riding up with her outstretched arm. My mother was quiet on the way to the bus stop and didn't have much to say to Denny as we rattled to Bantry. When my grandmother asked if we'd had a good day, she replied that God had sent her a test and she hoped she'd acquitted herself well.

EIGHT

At the end of the first week after her return from hospital my mother deteriorated suddenly, within a couple of hours. Doctor Molloy came; it might just be days now, he said to me. When I told my father he shook his head.

'She said she fancied a little ride out in the car last night.'

'I don't think that'll be possible now.'

'Should I call off Con and Una d'you think?'

His brother and his wife were due to visit. I was thinking that he would need them after she died; it had crossed my mind that he might even move to live near them, forty miles away in Waterford.

'I'd let them come; they've probably set out by now anyway. Mum's always been fond of Una.'

The relationship had been very much one of munificent benefactress (my mother) and grateful recipient (Una). Like a lot of people in rural Ireland in the fifties and sixties, Una thought that if you lived in England you must be rolling in money. It was a small farm that she and my uncle ran and they didn't appear to run it very well. Letters from Con to my father spoke of constant debts and big bills for broken machinery. My father had once remarked that all Con grew successfully was grass. Una would write separately to my mother about the terrible price of food, medical bills, and clothing. They swapped details of the menopause and gynaecological problems. Una was impressed by my mother's free

125

access to medical care and the fact that she was taken shopping in a car. The boxes of clothes that my mother despatched were evidence that England was the land of plenty. I used to think that Una was the kind of woman my mother might have been if she'd stayed in Ireland; pious, unsophisticated, fairly content with her lot.

My father and I had worked out a kind of routine. He had a mid-morning nap every day on my bed in the spare room while I spent time with my mother or, if she was asleep, prepared lunch. In the afternoon I took a walk while he read to her, working through their back copies of *Ireland's Own*. We made dinner a joint effort; he dealt with the meat. I found that I was hungrier than I'd been for years. I ate huge portions and found space for packets of biscuits between meals. I felt guilty about this appetite of mine, especially when I saw my mother's tiny portions untouched on their plates and witnessed her daily diminishment. I felt disgustingly robust and full of life; a healthy face looked back at me in the mirror. When I walked, I strode along vigorously, aware of the blood flowing strongly through my veins.

Con and Una had arrived when I got back from that afternoon's walk. I heard Una's loud voice as I opened the door. She was sitting on the edge of my mother's bed, holding her rosary.

'Ah, Rory,' she said. 'Me and your mammy have just been saying a few decades together. Isn't that right, Kitty?'

My mother was looking a little brighter. ''Tis a great comfort to me, Una.'

'Sure of course it is, of course. Prayer's a great healer, so they say. There's been times I've prayed and those prayers have been answered. I'm sure your prayers are getting a special hearing, Kitty, the angel you've been to me over the years.'

'Oh, I only did what I could,' my mother said.

'You did great altogether. You're one of those special people. I don't know now what I'd have done without you at all. The times those boxes of clothes have arrived and I've fallen on my knees and thanked God for an angel of a sister-in-law! I've always said, Kitty darling, there's a golden seat waiting for you in heaven.'

I looked at my mother in case she found this upsetting, but she seemed more at ease than she'd been for days.

'And how are you yourself, Rory, are you keeping well? Still doing the therapy?'

'That's right. I'm fine, thanks, Una. Would you like a cup of tea?'

'That'd be lovely. Con and your daddy have just gone for a little dander up the road. We packed them off, didn't we, Kitty, so that we could have a chat.'

I left Una telling my mother about the special novena she'd been saying for her and put the kettle on. A vague bad temper had come over me and I chided myself because I knew why; I was resenting the fact that Una could console my mother in a way that wasn't open to me, in a way that meant so much to her. At that moment, I wished I was still a Catholic so that I could genuinely sit with her and say those litanies that brought her comfort:

> Lamb of God
> *Pray for us*
> Mother of mercy
> *Pray for us*
> Ark of the covenant
> *Pray for us*
> Star of the sea
> *Pray for us*

Prayer had always held a magical significance for her. There was no problem that couldn't be tackled by an appropriate invocation and if she couldn't find one already written for her purpose, she would compose one. She often contributed to the *Irish Post*, sending a note for their column headed 'special intentions' where you could share a prayer's proven effectiveness with others, or carry out your promise to publish a saint's help:

> 'A plea to Our Lady for intercession on behalf of a loved one who has money problems; say three Hail Marys and a Glory Be on four consecutive Fridays and your prayer will be answered. Thanks also to St Blaise who responded to the following and cured tonsilitis; "touch my sinner's throat with your blessed fingers and make me well in body and in mind for the sake of Jesus Christ our Lord, amen."'

I warmed my hands over the steaming kettle, aware of the barriers separating me from my mother and Una. They were formed by age, culture and education. By raising me in a Protestant country and giving me a schooling that prompted me to question given truths, my parents had opened up a route that led me away from the values they clung to. As a child, I had uncomfortably tried to bridge a chasm between home and public life. At home I listened to rebel ballads, stories of the famine – how Queen Victoria sent five pounds to Battersea Dogs' Home and a shilling to the starving Irish – the deeds of Wolfe Tone, Michael Collins and Dev, all enshrined in the fervour of a religious belief that had inspired a struggling nation. My mother didn't teach me nursery rhymes; she passed on the tunes she'd grown up with. Before I went to school I knew the words of 'Skibbereen', 'Brian o' Linn' and 'The Foggy Dew'. I liked to sing 'Brian o' Linn' while I was dressing:

> Brian o'Linn had no breeches to wear
> He got an old sheepskin to make him a pair
> With the fleshy side out and the woolly side in,
> 'They'll be pleasant and cool,' says Brian o'Linn.

'The Foggy Dew' was a good rousing chorus for bath time; I would slap the water, beating out the rhythm:

Right proudly high over Dublin town
   They hung out the flag of war,
'Twas better to die 'neath an Irish sky
   than at Suvla or Sud el Bar
And from the plains of Royal Meath strong men
   came hurrying through,
While Britannia's Huns, with their blazing guns
Sailed in through the Foggy Dew.

At school I tried to take my place amongst the children of
Britannia's Huns. I quickly dropped the infant brogue I'd
arrived with, learned to speak in a cockney accent, sang 'The
British Grenadiers' in music lessons, 'God Save Our Gracious
Queen' at assembly and studied the history of the Plantagenets,
Stuarts and Tudors. My life became strictly compartmentalized
as I worked out a survival strategy. I hid away all my knowledge
of bold Fenian men and Father Murphy from old Kilcormack
who'd put the cowardly yeomen to flight. When I wrote an
essay on Oliver Cromwell I did not include the received
wisdom that he had a coal-black heart and was roasting
in the fires of hell for the foul crimes he'd committed in
Drogheda.

Despite their efforts, the Jesuits hastened my exit from the
faith. Their cerebral English Catholicism couldn't hold a
candle to my mother's rich bank of superstitions. In comparison, theirs was a delicate, watered-down variety that inspired
doubt in me. I had evolved into a hybrid creature and the
truth was that as an adult I was at home in neither country;
in England I often felt markedly Irish and in Ireland I often
felt reservedly English. I was a cultural schizophrenic. Perhaps
that was why Dermot had emigrated again, to adopt a national-
ity that he could make truly his own.

Una came into the kitchen as I spooned tea. She had always
looked a little like my mother; they were about the same height
and equally plump, or rather she was as plump as my mother
had once been. I found it hard to meet her eye.

129

'Ah Rory, 'tis a terrible time,' she whispered. 'And your poor father. What will he do without her? Sure they've been inseparable.'

'I suppose he'll carry on somehow.'

'I suppose. I've told her I'm having a mass said tomorrow.'

'She'll appreciate that, Una.'

'She's got you here anyway. She's missed you terrible since they moved back. You always understood her, that's what she told me. She said you've a bigger heart than Dermot.'

I stared at the brown stream of tea. Did she really think that or had it been something she said for Una's benefit, perhaps when Una was praising her relationship with one of her sons and my mother had felt the need to keep pace? It smacked of her usual mischief to me; I didn't want to dwell on it and I didn't want to be having this kind of conversation with Una.

'Oh,' I said lightly, 'I don't think you can compare heart sizes. Would you like cake?'

Both of my parents seemed cheered by their visit; they needed people of their own age about, I thought. When they'd gone I went in to my mother who was quickly slipping back into sleep.

'Biddy rang earlier, she's coming on the plane tomorrow evening. Did you hear me, Mum?'

She patted my hand and I turned to my father who'd filled her a fresh hot-water bottle.

'I was just trying to tell her that Biddy will be here tomorrow night.'

'Where will she stay? There's not space here, unless you kip down on the sofa.'

'I've told her I'll book a room at Kelly's b. & b.'

'Is she all right about that?'

'No problem, I've discussed it with her.'

I had decided to phone Biddy rather than write. She was still at the same house in Southend. Her accent was now completely anglicized. She'd said straight away that she'd come when I told her the news, although I'd wondered if she might change her mind when she'd had time to think it over.

'I'm glad she's coming,' my father said. 'It's best to settle up what you can. You shouldn't take an argument to the grave.' His shoulders shook, but he quickly composed himself. 'She's exhausted now,' he said, gently touching my mother's forehead. 'It all gets too much for her. She was never good with a lot of company. Do you recall, she'd get crotchety if we stood too near her?'

I nodded. 'Give me air, give me air!' she'd say, flapping her hands to create a space.

'Go and have a sit down,' I said to my father. 'I'll stay with her for a bit, then we'll do dinner.'

I leafed through a copy of *Ireland's Own*, remembering how I used to tease her about the parochial nature of the stories; 'Galway dog barks twice during trip to shops,' I'd pretend to read, or 'Cork woman loses five pence in park; Guards alerted.' She would sniff and remark that I was as clever as Cuttabags. I could never establish the identity of Cuttabags, he or she was a mystery to this day.

I held her hand for a few minutes; it was cool and papery. There was a new smell in the room, a sour odour that I hadn't noticed before, like curdled milk.

She woke at nine o'clock and called out. My father went in and spoke to her. I was watching the TV news but I turned the sound lower.

'She wants a breath of fresh air,' he said to me, appearing in the doorway. 'I told her it's cold out, but she's insisting.'

I followed him into the bedroom. She looked bleary but intent.

'I want to go out in the garden, just for a couple of minutes.'

'Would the morning do? It's cold.'

'Now, I want to now.'

'Right. I'd better carry you then, and Dad, you'd better take a chair out.'

'Take me Captain's chair.'

'Right you are, Kitty, I'll get it.'

I helped her to sit up against the bed frame, then slowly moved her legs around to the edge of the mattress as the nurse had demonstrated. Her shins were mottled, the skin drying. She balanced, a hand propped at either side of her. I found a chunky cardigan and put it on over her nightdress, buttoning it up to her neck. Then I pulled a pair of the thick grey walking socks I'd brought with me onto her legs and fetched her slippers. She wouldn't make the fashion catwalk this season, I told her, cocooning her in a blanket.

'A hat now,' I said, turning to the chest of drawers.

'No. I want to feel the air on me head.'

I was about to say that she might catch cold, but then realized the insignificance of that possibility. 'Okay. Now I'm going to count to three, then I'll lift you.'

She was a featherweight in my arms. I had never thought that I would feel my mother's bones. My father had switched the outside light on; the previous owners had had it installed, my parents would never have considered such a luxury themselves. I placed her in the chair that he'd positioned by her herb garden. She tilted her head back.

'The air's lovely,' she said.

'Look at the moon, it's a crescent.' I drew its shape with my finger.

'Did Con have much news?' she asked my father.

'Oh, the usual class of thing; banjaxed tractors, foot and mouth, scrapie, BSE . . . the sheep's in the meadow, the cow's in the corn.'

She sighed. 'Con's no farmer.'

'He's not. Maybe I should have stayed and run the place.'

'What would that have been like, I wonder?'

I'd moved aside to stargaze. For a moment it felt like the old life, when I used to visit before; my parents chatting in the evening gloom, my mother's voice lilting, the whiff of my father's cigarette on the breeze. They would be discussing what to plant next, the strange way the forsythia hadn't done well this year, their suspicion that the man who delivered the

132

turf was overcharging them, the odd manner of the doctor's receptionist. I touched the cold wall of the cottage; a sense of despair nudged me for the first time. Up until now I had been so busy, wrapped up in the details of the sickroom, getting a commode delivered, fielding phone calls and visitors, trying to make sure she was comfortable. This sudden taste of what had been and would soon vanish forever was too unexpected and shocking. I pressed my fingers into the wall, hard, hard.

'Take me back in, Rory,' she said weakly. 'Give me a bit of me rosemary first.'

I bent down beside her and picked some, folding it in the hand she presented at the tip of the blanket. I could see she was exhausted. My father followed us in with the chair, saying that he was sure there'd be a frost, it was almost a certainty.

I unwrapped her from the blanket and put her back in bed. She said to leave the thick socks on.

'Did ye say Angela's coming tomorrow?' she asked.

'No, Biddy, your sister.'

'I thought Angela might come. I thought she'd want to see me.'

She and Angela had enjoyed a mutual dislike from the first day they'd set eyes on each other. She'd accused Angela of taking me away from the church, even though I'd left it five years before I met her. I suppose it had eased her mind to decide that I'd been lured from the true faith instead of abandoning it.

'I'm divorced from Angela,' I said, but she was mumbling about her mother again; there had been milk spilt in the well, she said, and she'd got the blame but it had been Nellie who'd done it. She caught my hand.

'I want to be buried with me mother,' she whispered.

'In Bantry?'

'That's it.'

I felt sweat on my neck. The sour smell from the bed and the heat from the fire were making me dizzy.

'But you've got a grave picked out with Dad,' I whispered

133

back, looking behind me to check that he couldn't overhear us.

'She was a good mother, a good mother,' she said, rubbing her lips together and moving her legs restlessly. ' 'Twas Nellie did the milk, so 'twas.'

She quietened then, seeming to settle. I went to phone Dermot, to tell him it was time to fly back.

The Same Blood

In the spring of 1990 my father pulled a muscle in his back while he was lifting a bag of compost. I was staying with my parents at the time. We were giving the garden a rejuvenating work-over of hoeing and feeding. My mother was trimming with the secateurs, snipping away at dead branches and cossetting the magnolia she'd planted the previous year. I'd told my father not to touch the heavy bags, but he said that it was what he did all the time I wasn't around to help and there was life in the old dog yet. His muscle pinged as he bent down and he was in agony for a couple of days. I massaged his bony back and applied frozen peas, keeping my mother at bay with her hot poultices, rubbing alcohol and unguents. He improved gradually and was able to move about less gingerly, but still needed to take it easy.

On the third morning after his mishap my mother called to me as I was finishing breakfast. She'd been outside since before I got up, digging potato trenches. I'd lain in bed, hearing the rhythmic slice of the spade and the rattle of stones as she'd thrown them into a heap. Her voice, carrying on the early morning air, warned the cats to keep out of her way or she'd give them the order of the boot. The previous night she'd wound an elastic bandage around her stomach and announced that she was well and truly done for; her guts were rumbling like an express train and we may as well check the insurance policy and measure her up now. She'd swallowed half a jar of bicarbonate of soda and dragged herself to bed. Obviously, some kind of miracle had taken place overnight.

I took my cup of tea and went out to find her; she was sitting on a stool near the back door, balancing her right foot

135

over her left thigh and rubbing an old cheese grater against the ball of the foot.

'Don't tell me,' I said, 'you're out of cheddar.' I peered down at the feathery flakes of skin on the concrete. 'No; parmesan, I think.' She could still amaze me; this was a little foible I hadn't witnessed before.

' 'Tis the only thing that helps me corns,' she said, grating furiously.

'That isn't the grater you actually use in the kitchen, is it?' I waited nervously for her reply; last night we'd had cauliflower cheese, the cauliflower later being blamed for her gaseous intestinal spasms.

'Don't be an eejit. 'Tis an ould one I found in the cupboard.'

'You ought to be careful not to nick your skin. That thing's rusty. You could end up with blood poisoning and then corns would be the least of your troubles.'

'Yerra, ye needn't worry about that. There's enough hard skin here to keep me going for weeks. It makes walking pure purgatory.'

'You can buy special plasters for corns, to soften them.' I looked down at my cooling tea; I seemed to have lost my taste for it.

'Them ould things are useless, they come off. I do this and then I soak them. Wait 'til you get them, then you'll be sorry you weren't more sympathetic.'

'I am sympathetic. I'm just not sure that's the best way to tackle them.'

'Oh, ye and yeer science, ye think ye have the answers for everything. It's not many corn plasters me poor ould mother had.'

'Ah, but did she have corns?'

She looked up at me, stumped for a moment. Then she wielded the grater again, saying, 'Ah ye should have been on the stage, ye're such a comedian. They must miss ye at the London Palladium.'

I moved away from the scene of skin shaving, expecting her

to draw blood. It was a still, warm day with just a hint of breeze. The garden looked new, uncloaked. The faint growl of a tractor came from a few fields away and a wren darted by the hedge, watched carefully by the ginger cat. I closed my eyes and raised my face to the sun wondering, as I sometimes did when I stood on this spot, what my life might have been if instead of emigrating and meeting in London, my parents had settled in this house.

There was a parallel universe that crouched in my imagination, one where I had attended school in Fermoy, maybe gone to university in Cork or Dublin. What kind of person would I have become? If I'd grown up in Ireland, perhaps I would have headed for the priesthood, and be the Reverend Father Keenan tending to his faithful flock. Instead of being agnostic, divorced and childless, I might have married an Irish woman and made a success of my marriage for the glory of God, producing freckle-faced children. Or, of course, I could have turned out to be one of those men who never leave the family fireside; I could be living now with the Mammy and Daddy and going to dances in Fermoy but deciding that no girl could give me the kind of home comforts I got in the cottage above the valley. Maybe I would have emigrated, as daunted by the lack of prospects in Ireland as many of its youth, trained as a physiotherapist in London and be living much the same life as I did now. I liked to tease myself with the possibilities of those other Rorys.

One of the cats had been scratching at the newly-sprinkled compost, scattering it over the edge of the border. I kicked it back under a shrub. A clump stuck to my shoe and I shook it, the movement taking me back to when we used to go gathering horse manure. Many of my childhood Sunday afternoons had been spent stacking carrier bags of dung in the car boot. My mother would decide that the roses needed a good feed and we'd head off to Wormley Woods near Epping, where there were bridle paths and stables dotted around the countryside. My father would carry a trowel while she stuffed the carrier bags in her pocket. She would point as soon as she saw a pile of dung, then check to see if it might still be warm; the fresher the better, she maintained. Then my father would scoop while she held a bag open and eventually we would return to the car laden with garden nourishment. If she saw a horse in front of us she would slow down, saying we might as well hang about a bit, it would probably do its business and then we'd hit the jackpot. Once, during a period when the car was out of action, she had taken me to Epping on the Green Line bus, anxious that the roses were being deprived for too long. On the return journey we sat clutching several steaming bags each and, although there were plenty of passengers waiting at the stops, we had loads of space to ourselves.

The sawing noise behind me stopped and she knocked the grater on the ground to clean it.

'That's better,' she said, examining her feet, 'I feel pounds lighter. Now, there was something I wanted to ask ye. Would ye take me out for the day?'

'What, today?'

'Yes. I asked yeer father and he wouldn't mind. He can have a rest. I've left him a bit of soup for his dinner.'

'It's okay with me. Where do you want to go?' This was an odd request. Usually, if I suggested an outing she refused, saying she didn't want to be racketing around the countryside like a giddy goat.

She stood up. 'I'll give ye directions,' she said airily. 'I'll just be a few minutes. See if yeer father wants a cup of tea before we go.'

She vanished inside. Her grated skin lay in a little heap. I shifted it with my foot, dumping it by a spread of forget-me-nots where it could join the great recycling scheme of things.

My father still had tea in the big flask she'd given him earlier. The flask had a knitted cover in green, white and gold that she'd made for it. 'You're off out then?' he asked, resting his book on his knee.

138

'Looks like it.' I donned my jacket and checked that I had my wallet.

'That's good. Your mother could do with a little break. She still misses her old London cronies.'

'I always *offer* to take you out when I come.'

'Ah, but that's not the same as herself *deciding* to go,' he remarked knowingly.

She appeared from their bedroom. She had a clean dress and cardigan on, a pair of dark brown stockings held up with the home-made garters she wore, low-heeled lace-up shoes and she was carrying her voluminous handbag with the big brass clasp. She'd put on her thin-strapped watch; it caught my eye because she so rarely wore any ornamentation.

'You're going to be time-keeping then?' I asked, lifting her wrist.

'Oh, I don't want to be stopping out late; ye might turn into a pumpkin. Now, Dan, the soup's in the saucepan and the bread's in the cupboard.'

'I think I can manage a drop of soup,' my father observed, obviously dying to get on with his book.

'Tarra then, ducks,' she yodelled, mimicking a woman who used to live in our street in Tottenham and who could be heard bidding her husband goodbye at their front door every morning. She picked up her blackthorn stick which was propped by the front door and gave the window behind my father a farewell rattle with it as she passed.

In the car we had our usual tussle over her seat belt. She didn't want to wear it; I insisted.

'It cuts into me. It makes me feel all trussed up like a sack of spuds,' she protested as I clicked it into place.

'You'll get used to it. Now, where to?'

'Ye'll want the road to Cork first.'

'And then?'

'Oh, I'll direct ye on from there.' She sat back and folded her arms, her stick tucked in beside her.

'This is a mystery tour, is it?'

139

She tapped the side of her nose with a forefinger. I had the feeling that she'd been planning this outing for some time, waiting for the right day. The request might have been made casually, but I'd never known her get ready so quickly to leave the house; usually her purse was lost, her shoes unpolished, her bag not hanging where she'd last left it.

'Isn't the spring lovely?' she said as we joined the main Cork road. Her voice was light and optimistic.

'It is. It lifts your spirits after winter.'

'I always loved the spring the best. Don't drive too fast, now.'

'Give me a clue where we're going,' I said, 'animal, vegetable or mineral?'

But she wouldn't be drawn. She started to hum a jig, doing little steps with her feet.

'Let's have a verse of an ould song,' she suggested.

'Okay, which one?'

'"The Galway Shawl", that's a grand air, me father used to sing it when me mother put her bonnet on to go to the market.' She started and I joined in:

> In Arranmore in the county Galway
> One pleasant evening in the month of May,
> I spied a colleen, she was fair and handsome
> Her beauty fair took my breath away.
> She wore no diamonds, no costly perfume,
> No paint or powder, no none at all
> But she wore a bonnet with ribbons on it
> And around her shoulders a Galway shawl.

'Mind,' my mother said when we'd finished, 'there was no danger that he'd buy me mother diamonds or perfume. She lived hand-to-mouth, the poor creature, she was lucky to have her bonnet.'

'What did your father do?'

'God knows. He was missing half the time and when he was with us he'd had a skinful. I remember though, the time he took meself and John-Jo to Ballyboy Races. He had a flutter on a horse called "Bantry Bugler" and didn't he win five pound. Oh, then he was in the best of tempers and he bought us glasses of gooseberries and gave us a penny each. I got meself a stick of Peggy's Leg and a blue balloon. Sure I was beside meself completely, we weren't used to things like that.'

'Do you think your mother saw any of the money?'

'Yerra I doubt if she saw a pound. Didn't he get roaring drunk and we had to get a lift home on a pony and trap. He was like yer one in the story; when he was good he was very, very good and when he was bad he was horrid.'

'We're near Cork,' I pointed out.

'Take the road to Bandon when ye see it, that'll be fine and dandy.'

As we approached Bandon she said that she was starved with the hunger and we should have a bite to eat.

'Is it much further?' I asked as we went into a pleasant-looking café.

'Oh no, we've the back of it broke. Now, d'ye think they do chips?'

They did and she had a plate of them with two fried eggs while I chose soup.

'Remember that time in Cork when you threw tea on the table?' I said.

She looked askance. 'I did not! What makes ye say that?'

'Yes you did. You didn't like the service or the food so you *accidentally* spilled the tea. There was a matter of some jam, too, as I recall.'

She shook her head. 'Ye must be thinking about something else. Sure I wouldn't do such a thing.'

I dropped the subject and tucked into my soup. She made short work of the egg and chips and ordered a chocolate éclair. The young waitress was friendly and efficient.

'She's a nice girl,' my mother said through a mouthful of cream. 'She's the type would suit you.'

'Oh, is she?'

141

' 'Tisn't good for a man to be on his own.'

'I think I should find out a bit more about someone first though; she might have skeletons in the cupboard or a mad husband in the attic.'

'I don't suppose there's any chance of ye and Angela getting back together?'

I could never work out, when she made that kind of remark, if she'd genuinely blotted out reality or was trying to draw me on the subject of my personal life. 'I shouldn't think so; last time I heard from her she was planning to marry again.'

My mother shook her head and dabbed up the last of her cake. ' 'Tisn't natural, all these broken marriages and marrying again. It flies in the face of God.'

I rarely ventured into conversations on such topics with her, but the unexpected shape of the day had relaxed me.

'Marriage was never meant to last as long as it's supposed to now.'

'How d'ye mean?'

'People live much longer. In the past, an average marriage lasted maybe twenty years. People died off. Look at your own parents; your mother was only married for a comparatively short time.'

'That's not the point,' she said; 'while ye're married ye should work at it.'

'Well, not everyone can.'

'Put yeer trust in Our good Lord on high, pray to him daily and ye can do anything,' she said, sitting back with her cup.

Our conversations were programmed to wander in this hopeless circle. What was it a friend had once said to me? Never try to argue with a religious zealot, it's like struggling through a maze.

'D'ye know,' she said to me suddenly, 'I could just smoke a cigarette. Would they have one, d'ye think?'

'What, just one?'

'Yes. Ask the waitress.'

I'd known her have the odd cigarette before, at whist drives or with her sherry at Christmas. It signalled that she was taking things easy, feeling maybe a little daring. I approached the waitress who didn't bat an eyelid at my request, but came back with a king-size cigarette and a box of matches. My mother lit up and took inexpert small puffs, barely inhaling. She crossed her legs and propped her elbow on the table, holding the cigarette in the air. She was like a teenager, full of bravado.

'Let's make tracks now,' she said when she'd half smoked it, 'or the day will be gone. Ye take the road to Rosscarbery from here.'

We headed off with the windows wound down. I could sense her growing excitement as we approached her secret destination. She gestured at the huge signs proclaiming road improvements funded by grants from the European Economic Community.

'This has all changed entirely since I was a girl. The roads used to be full of ould potholes, ye had to be careful not to twist yeer ankle. God bless and save them European fellas!'

A couple of miles outside Rosscarbery she told me to stop. 'Let me get me bearings now, 'tis years since I was here.' She frowned and held up a finger, her lips moving silently. 'Go right up here, then there's a road to the left.'

I moved off, driving slowly. We cruised for ten minutes while she clutched at the dashboard, growing anxious. There was no sign of a road to the left.

'Saint Anthony help us,' she said. 'Everything looks different, I can't picture where we are. Stop at that place up ahead, look.'

She was opening the car door before I'd pulled up, and beetled along the path of a cottage set back from the road. I watched her knocking, then stepping forward as a woman opened the door. There was some conversation. The woman stepped down the path with my mother, gesticulating. As I watched, a cat padded around from the side of the house, disappeared through the front door and reappeared after a minute with a large chop flopping from its jaws. It shot off out of view. It was like a silent film; the woman pointing, my mother nodding, the cat sneakily seizing its opportunity while its owner, her back turned, was absorbed in another matter. I started to laugh. I was still laughing when my mother got back in the car.

'What ails ye?' she asked.

I shook my head. 'Tell you later.' It was a story she'd relish on the way home. 'Do you know where we are or is the mystery trip continuing?'

'That one told me they changed the road signs about ten years ago. We go on up here, turn right, then left. She was very interested in who we were, the nosy ould scut. Did ye see her eyeballs out on stalks taking a good gander at the car? I pretended I was over from England and gave her a false name. I'd say she's the talking newspaper for the parish.'

'What name did you say?'

'Flanagan.'

I pressed my lips together. She was priceless and without shame.

After a few minutes my mother said, 'That's it! Drive on past a bit.' We passed a small unremarkable cottage with a peeling yellow door.

'Stop now!' she commanded after fifty yards. She pulled down the mirror on the sun visor and neatened her hair. 'Wait here for half an hour, then turn around and come to that house we passed. Keep yeer mouth shut when ye're in there and don't be giving any information. Just follow me own lead. Have ye got that?'

I nodded, a bit dazed. My mother headed back up the road; I watched her disappear in my rear-view mirror. I pulled the car in close to the side and got out to stretch my legs. The silence was tangible. What was she up to, I wondered? Whatever it was, it had fired her with a rare energy and made her a congenial companion. I didn't mind her waywardness and her orders today, they were entertaining.

As instructed, I turned the car and presented myself at the

yellow door. A middle-aged woman in a see-through purple plastic mac and wearing pink rubber gloves and a shower cap on her head opened it.

'Ah come in,' she said, 'yeer mother's here. Did ye get yeer Aspirin all right?' She took me straight into a kitchen that smelled of boiling cabbage.

My mother was sitting at the table and nodding at me encouragingly. 'I told Ita ye'd had to go off and get something for yeer headache.'

I played along. 'Oh yes, I'm a bit better now.'

'And ye're Rory?' asked Ita, putting her gloved hands on her hips.

'That's right.'

'Me youngest,' my mother added, 'the last of me little nest.'

'Tay?' offered Ita.

'Please,' I said.

'Ye'll have to drink up quickly, Rory, so ye can be back for that appointment,' my mother said significantly, consulting her watch.

'Yes, of course.'

'What time do ye have to be back?' Ita was pouring me syrupy brown tea from a huge soot-encrusted pot. Her mac rustled as she moved.

I took the mug, wondering if my mother had interrupted her in the middle of cleaning or whether her get-up was the day-time fashion in this part of the county. I did a quick mental calculation. 'Four,' I said.

'And have ye a fast car?' she asked.

'Not so fast, but not too bad,' I equivocated. I was doing pretty well, I thought, hoping that the nature of my appointment wasn't going to be pursued.

'Ah well, 'tis good enough for ye to have the wheels. I'm stuck for a bit of ould transport out here.'

The tea was like treacle. I felt it slithering down and sticking to my stomach walls. Ita rummaged in a tin and brought out a pale shop-bought sponge cake with fluorescent orange icing.

'Here,' she said, hacking off a hunk and presenting it to me in her gloved hand, 'make an impression on that.'

She seemed truculent, I thought. The rubber glove was grimy and through a hole in the tip of one of the fingers I'd spied a dirty nail. I bit into the unwanted cake. It was stale but mushy, a fascinatingly awful combination. The icing exploded in a chemical extravaganza on my tongue.

'And the children, Ita, how are they?' my mother enquired. I noticed that she had avoided the cake and was toying with her tea. I suspected that before my arrival she'd offered me up as a man who was always desperate for a bit of iced sponge.

'Oh, the usual. Sarah's gone to England where the streets are paved with gold. Tommy's at an agricultural college.'

'That's grand.'

'Maybe. I did what I could for them anyway.'

There was a dank, gloomy atmosphere despite the fire and the rattling kettle. A huge open pot stood on an Aga, steaming steadily; I spotted the knobbly end of a bacon knuckle sticking out of it and guessed that was where the cabbage also lurked. I eyed my mother and she pushed her chair back.

'It was grand seeing ye, Ita. Sure the time's flown altogether.'

Ita scratched under her shower cap. It had a dolphin motif around the crown and her movement seemed to set them swimming. She stood at the door as we started the car, her hands stuck in her pockets. My mother gave a cheery wave, then ran a hand across her brow once we'd accelerated away.

'Bless all the saints in heaven, that was hard going.' Her tone held satisfaction, though. 'Ye did grand, Rory; a real Larry Olivier.'

'Are you going to tell me who she was?'

'Only if ye promise not to say anything to anyone about her.'

'Not even Dad?'

'No.'

I shrugged. 'Okay.'

146

She lowered her voice and glanced around, as if there might be an eavesdropper in the back of the car. 'That's Nellie's youngest girl, Ita.'

I thought back to Nellie's neat living-room in Liverpool and the way she'd arranged the food in serving dishes. 'But didn't Nellie have her children here adopted through the nuns?'

'She did. But me mother persuaded them to give her Ita after Nellie had taken off to England. She went up to the convent and begged. The nuns hadn't found parents for her so they agreed.'

'Hang on a minute. Did Nellie know?'

'No. Me mother put Ita with a simple ould cousin of hers in Durrus who said nothing because she got some of the allowance. But she went down there to see her regular and looked after her as if she was her own.'

'Did Ita never want to meet her mother?'

'She didn't need to.' There was a pause. 'She thought Nana was her mother.'

I drove on, feeling Ita's poisonous cake giving me the head-ache I was supposed to have had previously.

'I just wanted to see her,' my mother mused. ' 'Twas the first time in years and I won't bother again. I promised me mother I'd never spill the beans about her. That's why you've got to stay quiet.'

'Why would it matter now? Your mother's dead and Nellie's dead. Dad could know; he's hardly likely to rush off and tell Ita.'

'A promise is a promise,' my mother said firmly. 'Me mother, God rest her soul, wouldn't be aisy in her grave if she thought I'd spread the word. I've only told ye because I know ye're a dark horse. I can never get any information from ye.'

We bypassed Cork. I pondered on the huge capacity my mother's family had for flirting with deep plots and shadowy deeds.

'How come she wasn't there when Nana was buried?'

147

'She was in hospital having Tommy. I sent her a mass card. 'Twas she put up the grave stone.'

I was piecing it together. 'So she thinks you're her sister although in fact you're her aunt.'

'That's right; well, a half-sister. Nana told her she had a different father, she was illegitimate.'

'She was. Is.'

'Yes.'

'It's just that she didn't know her true mother.'

'Wisha, Nana was her true mother; didn't she pluck her from the orphanage and keep her and feed her.'

'So I was there as a nephew, but I'm actually a cousin.'

'I suppose. I hadn't thought of it like that. Sure what matter, 'tis all the same blood.' My mother nudged me. 'That ould cake had seen better days.'

'I liked the shower cap.'

'I don't know what me mother would say if she saw her now. Stop in Fermoy, I want to get some of them oaty biscuits.'

'Where are we going to say we've been if Dad asks?'

She leaned towards me. 'Around and about the countryside, looking at me ould haunts. That's only a biteen of a white lie.'

I waited for her outside the shop in Fermoy, rubbing my tender temples and regretting that icing. You could say this for my mother; life with her was rarely dull.

NINE

Biddy's plane was an hour late. I drank over-brewed coffee at the airport and watched landing lights descend through the darkness. Any delay now made me twitchy. My mother had slept a good deal of the day, taking sips of drinks when she woke. At times she was alert, but mostly she looked distant. Father Brady had called again, this time administering the last rites. The nurse had delivered huge nappy-like incontinence pads. My father said he'd see to those. He was tired and worn-looking. My mother had been restless throughout the previous night. He'd had to call me at one point because she was trying to get out of bed; there was the dinner to make, she was saying, the chops would be burning, you had to keep them on a low heat.

'I'll look after the chops, Kitty,' he'd told her, holding her arms.

'Dermot, Rory?' she said, 'is your father there?'

'I'm here, Kitty, it's me.'

'No, he's having an operation. The poor man's being pinned together.'

'That's all over now,' I'd said. 'He's here, Dad's here.'

We'd settled her back, straightening the tangled sheets.

'He's a hopeless saver, he can never keep a bit of money, never a bit at all. There's the insurance man to pay.' She'd tried to sit up again. 'Will one of ye pay him?'

'I will, I'll pay him now,' I'd lied, and that seemed to satisfy her.

I wanted my father to swap places with me and get some rest in my room, but he refused. He'd have plenty of time, too much time to rest when she'd gone, he'd said. I'd woken every hour, listening in the darkness. He was up most of the night, either seeing to her or making tea. At one point I heard him talking. I got up and tiptoed from my room. He was kneeling on the living-room floor, praying, a lighted candle in front of the statue of the Sacred Heart. At dawn he was in the garden, wandering the path and smoking. I took a scarf out to him.

'Here, have some sense, your chest is weak.'

'Thanks. She's sleeping a bit now. Maybe she feels safer with the light.'

'You were right about the frost.' A clear, bright morning was breaking, carrying the kind of cold that was hard on my father's drying joints.

'I was, so.' He inhaled deeply. 'She was a bit like that the night before you were born. Not confused, of course, but restless. 'Twas very hot and she couldn't get comfortable. She had me fetching iced water every five minutes.' He scuffed at the hard ground. 'Fifty-one years we've been together. Did I ever tell you how I met her, at Hyde Park Corner?'

'She told me. You were listening to the man from the Flat Earth Society.'

'That's it. She pushed in front of me. Her hair was shiny and she was wearing this sort of scarf; 'twas the colour of it caught my eye, a class of a cloudy blue. Very jaunty, she looked. When I heard her accent I was delighted. London was a lonely kind of a place.'

Jaunty; I could picture her, elbowing her way forwards to get a better look, her hair brushed until it sparked, her scarf done in a stylish bow. In their wedding photo she looked very modish; slim, in a dark fitted suit with a tilted hat and a spray of lily of the valley on her lapel. My father held himself formally, his expression reserved, but she smiled confidently at the camera, her gaze direct.

I shivered in my dressing-gown.

'You go on in,' he said. 'I'll just finish this fag. I'm often out here at this hour, watching the world go by. There's a robin pops out around now, I keep a bit of bread for him in my pockets.'

I bought minty chewing gum to take away the taste of the coffee and drifted back to the ground floor of the terminal. Biddy's plane was due in ten minutes, a monitor said. I circled the tall bronze statue of the hurler inside the main door, recalling the barn-like young man my mother had attempted to entertain when he'd stayed with us one night in Tottenham. A hurling team from Kilkenny had come over to take on a local group of enthusiasts, The Chuchulains, in a kind of lads of Erin vs. exiles match. Father Corcoran had masterminded the event; in his youth he'd played the game for Ireland and had an array of silver cups in the presbytery. We so rarely had anyone staying the night that we all felt jittery. My mother, of course, having rushed to the front of the queue with an offer of hospitality when overnight bunks were requested, had come home and panicked; what would this fella be like, would he snore, would he expect towels in the room, would he be a country eejit with no sense and dirty habits?

The day of the match, a Saturday, I came down for breakfast to a sight so unusual I rubbed my eyes in disbelief, wondering if my first illicit puff of a cigarette the night before had affected my brain. My mother was on her knees with a scrubbing brush, cleaning the kitchen floor.

Furniture had been dusted and polished, the Hoover was out, windows sparkled, piles of clothes were cleared away, the stack of ironing that had been festering damply for a month had been completed. When I made some comment on how nice the front-room looked she wiped her brow and said she wasn't having any fella from Kilkenny going home and saying that a Cork woman didn't know how to entertain a guest. Her

151

home county's reputation was on the line and wouldn't be found wanting.

My father, like me, took no interest in hurling or any sport, but we were pestered by her into going to the match. She couldn't possibly attend, she had far too much to do, but we were to take a tin full of ham sandwiches she'd made for half-time.

'Do they have half-time in hurling matches?' my father asked, being difficult because he'd planned to spend Saturday afternoon with his vegetables.

'They must do,' she said. 'They always have half-times with them things.'

'Have we got to bring him home afterwards?' I asked.

'Well, of course! How else would he find his way here? Now, will I use the willow pattern plates for dinner?'

My father gunned the car, muttering that you'd think the Shah of Persia was visiting with the fuss that was being made. At the school field where the match was being held, we handed the sandwiches to one of the women who was running the refreshments stall and looked about us. Burly men swinging hurling sticks were running around and thwacking balls to each other in a warm-up. Children skittered along the edges of the field, screaming encouragement. There were cries of 'Up Kilkenny!' and 'Come on now, Chuchulains!' My father and I eyed each other.

'How long will the match last?' he asked a spectator.

'Oh, about two hours in all, with presentations at the end.'

'I could drop you at the library and head off to the allotment for an hour, then pick you up. We'd be back to get your man.'

I nodded, grinning. 'I'll make sure I find out the score at the end.'

'And ask about any incidents or injuries. We'll need a watertight story.'

We arrived back as the cup was being presented to the Kilkenny team and the runner-up shield to The Chuchulains.

Father Corcoran boomed through the loudspeaker that anyone hosting a player for the night should report to the school
hall to pick up their guest. Our man turned out to be one
Kevin Mullen, a lumbering, shy youth of twenty who had
collected most of the soft mud from the playing field on his
body. We ferried him home, trying hard to make conversation,
but his vocabulary consisted of 'yes' and 'no' with the odd
'that's right' thrown in for excitement. A fetid, sweaty reek
filled the back of the car.

As he ploughed his way to our bathroom with his bag,
my mother watched clods of earth littering her newly-washed
floors.

'Lord God,' she muttered as the lock rasped on the bathroom door, 'I didn't know he was going to bring half the
pitch back with him.'

'Conditions were soft,' my father offered with a smirk.

The evening was a long, painful nightmare. My mother went
into social overdrive in an effort to draw Kevin out, talking
ten to the dozen, laughing heartily at her own witticisms and
pressing huge quantities of food on him. She had inserted her
teeth for the occasion, but shrinkage in her gums meant that
they slipped now and again, making a clicking noise. She would
cover her mouth with her napkin to reinsert them, shoving
upwards with a grimace and continuing to talk at her frozen
guest. It hardly seemed possible that he could become more
withdrawn, but he did; his head tucked into his shoulders, he
adopted a blank expression and, losing the power of speech
completely, made strangled noises in his throat.

He escaped to bed at half-nine when my father took pity
on him, saying he must be exhausted after the journey and
the game. I had never seen such gratitude in a man's eyes; he
was up the stairs in a flash.

'Well,' my mother said, flushed with her efforts, 'can you
beat that! What kind of a gom is he at all?'

'Ah, he's just shy,' my father told her.

'Shy! Ignorant, ye mean. To think of the trouble I went to

getting the place ready and not a civil word out of him. Anyone would think we were torturing him.'

In the morning, when my father went to call him, he'd fled. We heard later that he'd been waiting for the coach outside the church two hours early, at seven o'clock.

I touched the bronze hurler's knee, wondering if Kevin Mullen occasionally regaled his children with the story of the mad house he escaped from in London.

Biddy's flight was announced. As she came through the arrivals' door I saw that she'd hardly changed. She was a little stouter, but her hair was carefully dyed and her make-up skilful. She was a well-preserved woman, I thought. I waved to her as she looked through the crowd and wondered how I should greet an aunt I'd last seen over twenty years ago and who I'd parted from under a cloud. A handshake? A nod? A pat on the arm? She solved the problem for me by reaching up and tapping my cheek with her gloved hand.

'Aren't you tall, like your father,' she said.

'Hallo, Biddy. How was your flight?'

'Hot and crowded. How's Kitty?'

I told her about the deterioration as we headed for the car.

'Was it all very sudden, Rory?'

'Yes, and the cancer's moved fast.'

'It does, often. It did with Roy.'

I looked down at her. 'Roy's dead?'

'Oh yes, eight years ago. Bowel cancer.'

'I'm sorry, I didn't know.'

'I've only May left now, and she's emigrated to Florida with her family.'

'You live alone?'

'Yes. I've the house up for sale at the moment, it's too big for me. I don't know why I've stayed so long. Memories, I suppose.'

She looked around as we drove away from the airport, exclaiming about how much things had changed.

'How long is it since you've been in Ireland?'

'Oh, God, I can hardly remember; must be forty years. Roy would never come over; he thought if you were English you got shot as soon as you set foot here. After he died I thought about a visit, but I don't know . . . it's hard when you've been away so long.'

'Mum and Dad have been back ten years.'

'Ah, that's why she didn't reply to my letter.'

'You wrote to her?'

'One Christmas, about seven years ago. I sent it to Tottenham. Do you mind if I smoke?'

'No, go ahead.'

She lit up. 'I didn't know if I was a fool, writing. Roy was dead, and Danny. I was thinking that life's short and it was daft that my own sister wasn't talking to me, or vice versa, whichever it was; I was never sure.'

'You must have been very disappointed when she didn't reply.'

'I was and I wasn't. Kitty was never predictable.' She touched my arm. 'I don't mean that as any offence, now. It's just her nature.'

'I know.' If they had still been in Tottenham, would she have responded, I wondered? There was no knowing.

'You might get a shock when you see her,' I warned. 'She's very shrunken and pale.'

'I've seen it with Roy. I don't think there'll be any surprises.'

I changed gear, slowing down for the turn in the road.

'That's the cottage, you can just see the light. I was sorry to hear about Danny.'

'How did you know about him?'

'Nellie wrote and told us.'

'Ah. I still miss Danny. The hurt never goes.'

As I stopped the car she touched her lips nervously.

'She does know I'm coming?'

'I told her. But she's not always with it, she might have forgotten. She wanted you to come though, that's what she said.'

My mother was taking sips of warm milk from a spoon as we arrived. My father held the spoon to her mouth, saying, 'There you go, now, that's great, down the hatch.'

Biddy hung back, waiting by the fire until they'd finished. He came out to her, limping from the aches in his legs.

'Biddy,' he said, 'you were good to come all this way.'

She took his hand. 'She's the only sister I have left. It's good to see you, Dan, it's been too long.'

'Ah well . . . you're here now. Will you go in and see her?'

'I'll take Biddy in,' I said, seeing that he was swaying.

My mother's eyes were closed and her breath sounded hoarse. The room was warm and scented with the tall cinnamon-fragranced candle I'd bought. Biddy sat on a chair by the bed, shrugging her coat off.

'Kitty? Can you hear me, Kitty?'

My mother opened her eyes and focused as Biddy said her name again. She tightened her rosary beads in her hand, pulling at the edge of the pillow. A little of the milk had dripped onto it.

'I'm sad for Danny,' she said with difficulty, straining to project her voice, 'your loss.'

'It seems a long time ago now.'

'Where was he buried?'

'In Southend. With his books.' She looked at me. 'He taught English.'

My mother looked at me. 'Is Dermot on his way?'

'He's catching a plane tonight. He'll be here tomorrow.'

She gave a slight nod. 'I'm awful tired,' she said.

Biddy stood. 'We'll let you sleep. I'll see you again later.'

We sat by the fire, talking quietly, Biddy and my father puffing away. Biddy still worked part time as a secretary, in the same job she'd had for years. She belonged to a widows' club; they went on social outings and holidays together. Back in July they'd been to Madeira for two weeks. She was saving up for a second trip to Florida next year. I watched and listened, noticing her pale nail varnish. She was like many other carefully maintained English widows of her age. Sometimes they came to me for treatment after breaking bones or having hip replacements. They filled their days with part-time jobs, social outings, shopping, trips to see relatives. Biddy had successfully reinvented the penniless girl with a thick brogue who had left Ireland and her illegitimate offspring. I wondered how she and my mother could have turned out so different; then I thought of Dermot and nodded to myself.

TEN

That night my mother was less restless, but my father was up just as much, wakeful with his own relentless pain. I slept lightly, on the edge of fleeting, confused dreams that incorporated the sounds of his tea-brewing, his coughing and the rustling of his newspaper. Now and again I would open my eyes and stare into the darkness, making out shapes around me.

The spare room where I was staying was crammed with the things they had little use for but wouldn't get rid of. Some of the knick-knacks were reminders of the beardy fella days; a cuckoo clock, a pair of wooden butter shapers, several snuff boxes and a variety of chipped china jugs. A hat stand was jammed by the small window, blocking the light. On the walls around my bed hung several of Miss Diamond's artistic efforts, the picture of the holy family bought in Martha and Mary, a plaque of St Peter's that I had brought back from Rome, the old sepia-tinted photo of Dev that had been with them for ever and a brass shield with the Keenan coat of arms. My mother had always been a sucker for details of family lineage; like a lot of other Irish people she was convinced that we could trace our line to the High Kings of Ireland, who must have been an enormously prolific crew if they had as many direct descendants as were claimed.

The room smelled of mildew and the mattress held a dampness that the heat of my body never entirely subdued. My father had had a couple of odd-jobmen in tinkering with the back wall, but apart from drinking pints of tea and eating them out of biscuits these specialists hadn't effected any cure; dark patches of moisture still traced their way along the plaster like spreading stains. My parents had always seemed untroubled by the fabric of their houses. In Tottenham, a chunk of plaster had fallen from the kitchen ceiling and lain in the corner for five years before they thought of clearing it away and perhaps having the bulge above their heads looked at. When he heard talk of damp-proofing or double glazing my father laughed and said didn't all houses have damp, they were built on earth, and didn't all buildings need to breathe. My mother agreed, especially on the subject of double glazing, which she thought extremely unhealthy; she believed that air trapped in a house went stagnant and caused blood to go septic.

When I woke fully at seven I smelled the bacon my father was frying and my stomach turned over. I reached around the hat stand and opened the window for a few gulps of air. The day was dank and filled with low cloud; down in the hollow where Biddy was staying at the Kelly's B & B it would be misty.

My father was sitting with a cat on his lap and eating bacon trapped between two thick slices of bread. The cat was sniffing eagerly and was rewarded with a sliver of rind.

'She had a better night,' he confirmed. 'I wouldn't mind having a kip when I've finished this though, the missed sleep's catching up on me.'

'Go ahead. I'll fetch Biddy about ten. Dermot will be here sometime this afternoon.'

'Imagine, a house full. I can't get used to it not being the two of us. Just about now I'd take her in a cup of tea and tell her what the weather's like. She's always dreaded these kinds of days when it's hard to work outside.'

'What would she do?'

'Oh, listen to the wireless, do a bit of baking, doze, batter me into taking her to Fermoy. Write a few letters, maybe. She likes them old chat shows on TV.' He shook his head. 'At

159

least with me around she couldn't be up to moving a wall or rearranging the chimney stack.'

'Do you remember the day in Tottenham when she dug a pond out the back?'

'Oh Lord, don't be reminding me. An unholy mess that was! It took me a month to get the ground flat again.'

We were talking about her as if she'd already gone. In a way she had, edging her way from our lives, backing out of a door that was still open just a crack. Perhaps it was best to anticipate like this, gradually adjusting.

My father creaked his way to my still-warm bed. I looked in on my mother and saw that she was sleeping. Her face looked now like a little bird's, her cheeks shrunk away from her nose, throwing it into sharp relief. A song came into my head, one that I'd heard my grandmother sing:

> Oh her cheeks were like apples
> Her hair spun with gold
> And I followed her home
> Feeling aisy and bold.

When the nurse arrived I left her to see to my mother while I cleared up. In the kitchen I had to be careful not to fall into any of the traps my mother had laid for non-vigilant helpers. For reasons best known to herself she liked to swap things from their original containers into ones of her choice; for example, washing-up liquid was often to be found in a bottle labelled floor polish while bleach lurked in the washing-up liquid container. The floor polish might well have been poured into an old milk carton. So it went on; the permutations were endless and followed no discernible pattern. You had to stay alert with all senses sharp if you didn't want to be caught out. I had once scooped what I took to be pale margarine into a saucepan; when I turned back I saw that it was foaming. My mother had transferred a solid soap for woollens into the margarine tub. I never found the margarine; I settled for corn oil, remembering this time to sniff the attractive golden liquid before pouring, to check that it wasn't really all-purpose lubricant or bath fragrance. This morning I noticed that the white sugar my father heaped in his tea was stored in a jar marked Sea Salt. That was a particularly subtle move on her part as the two substances looked alike. I started to laugh uncontrollably, tears spilling down my cheeks, until my breaths turned to hiccups. I leaned gasping against the sink and it crossed my mind that never again in the course of my life would I meet anyone quite like her. At one time, I would have seized on that passing thought with relish. Now I knew that I would feel the lack of those very things that had maddened me. I stuck my head under the cold tap and gulped water.

The nurse looked at me kindly as she was closing her bag. I suppose she thought that I had been sobbing with grief. How could I have even started to explain? She touched my upper arm.

'Hardly any time now, I'd say. I don't like to be too definite but . . .'

'I know. My brother's on his way back.'

'Lots of people have been asking after your mother as I do my rounds.'

'We've had phone calls too, and people have called in.'

A woman I didn't know had dropped off a casserole. I assumed that most of these enquiries came from members of the church congregation; I was beginning to understand how an approaching death brought with it certain social niceties; neighbours knew the custom and relied on it.

When the nurse had gone the house was hushed, with an expectant air. I was reminded of mornings when I was little; my father would have gone off to work and I'd rattle around downstairs, waiting for my mother to get up. Sometimes she'd appear humming lightly, hurrying me into my clothes before we set off to the shops, stopping for sticky cakes in the tea-room and calling in to see a couple of her church cronies. Those were the best days, snug and easy. But if she'd lain in bed for a long time, she would thump heavily down the stairs and then I knew it was best to stay out of her way because nothing would be right and she might weep: she might bewail ever having come to England, ever having met my father. Her distress would fill me with a hammering panic, my throat growing salty. At times I crept away behind the back of a chair and cried, my nose becoming hot and blocked. Then my cheeks would feel like sandpaper and redden where I'd scratched them. I would stay in my tartan dressing-gown because I didn't know where my clothes were kept, doing jigsaws and counting on my brightly-coloured abacus. She would heave herself from the sofa to open a tin of beans or spaghetti for my lunch. In the late afternoon she'd help me dress, saying that I was a poor, thin creature; sure a strong gust of wind would blow me away. I would be swept up and clasped strongly to her chest as I tried to avoid being caught in the eye by the medals she wore or impaled on the sharp pin of one of her brooches.

I walked softly to her room. She was still deep in sleep. I crossed to the other side of the double bed and carefully lay down beside her, facing in towards her. Her mouth was so compressed that her lips had almost disappeared. I put a hand on her shoulder and laid my head on my hand. Sometimes, when I'd called up the stairs to her on good mornings, she'd shouted to me to come and join her in her parlour and I'd climbed, my tartan dressing-gown tassels swinging. Then she would throw back the covers and I'd tumble into the warm nest beside her, burrowing my cheek against her fat arm.

'Oh!' she'd say with a mock scream, 'yeer feet are like little cold mice,' and I'd run them up and down her legs, pretending to be a scuttling rodent.

We'd play 'I spy' for a while, then she'd plump up the pillows and give me a song, maybe 'The Grey Sheep'; that was one she'd often sung in the big houses where she worked. She'd launch into it during the early-morning hours, to get her spirits up while she was raking fires:

Oh I wish I was out with my sweetheart
On the peak of a mountain so high,
With no house or abode next or near us,
But the snow coming down from the sky;
My arms wrapped around him so tightly
That he never need fear for the cold
And I'd kiss him far into the night-time
With kisses worth silver and gold.

That was the verse I asked for; the bows on her nightdress would quiver as her bosom rose and fell. I'd get her to repeat it, sitting up in the bed and dramatizing as she sang, making a mountain peak with my hands, fluttering my fingertips to indicate falling snow, wrapping my arms around my body and kissing the air with puckered lips.

'Come on,' she'd say finally, shifting out of bed and causing the mattress to rise several inches, 'ye've me worn out with yeer shenanigans, it's time to shake the sauce bottle.'

Now I touched the thin skin of her face, feeling how still she was. Where are you, I wondered; are you here at all? I heard my father moving about and I got off the bed, smoothing the cover. He came through, combing his hair with his fingers.

'No change?'

'No. The nurse thinks it won't be long.'

He pulled up the chair. 'I'll stay with her now. She mustn't be left.'

I set off to fetch Biddy who was sitting with Mrs Kelly over the remains of a leisurely breakfast. Mrs Kelly had her own cup in front of her and there was an atmosphere of congenial chat.

'How is your dear mother this morning?' Mrs Kelly asked.

'About the same.'

'Ah, it's a hard time on all of you. Still, Biddy, isn't it good that you've come to heal the breach?'

Biddy nodded. 'I'm glad I had the chance. I have Rory to thank for phoning me.'

163

'Biddy's been telling me that your mother's people were from around Bantry,' Mrs Kelly said.

'That's right.' I could see that Biddy had been telling her a lot more as well. I thought how much my mother would dislike this; she'd say that Mrs Kelly had been ferreting for information, striking while the iron was hot to find out what she could. Then I gave myself a mental shake; what did it matter? My mother was beyond whatever real or imaginary motives Mrs Kelly might have and what use was this information to her anyway? 'It's good of you to put my aunt up at the last minute,' I said more agreeably, 'especially as it's out of season.'

'Oh, not at all, it's the least we can do. You'll be back tonight, Biddy?'

'Yes. Can I give you a ring to let you know what time?'

'Of course. No trouble at all.'

'I could have walked up really,' Biddy said as we got in the car, 'it's not so far.'

I looked at her thin shoes. 'It's a good twenty minutes and the lanes are wet.'

'She's a nice woman, that Mrs Kelly. I'd forgotten how genuine people are here. There's much more family feeling.'

'Have you any idea where John-Jo is these days?' I asked.

'No, I've not heard from him in years. I'd imagine he drank himself into an early grave, like our father.'

When I opened the door to the cottage my father was standing looking out of their bedroom. He lifted one hand, then dropped it slowly down.

'Your mother's gone. About five minutes ago.'

We followed him into the room. She lay just as I'd left her except that my father had placed her rosary in her hands. An open *Ireland's Own* lay on the chair. Biddy touched my father's arm, saying, 'Poor Kitty, ah poor Kitty.'

I stood at the foot of the bed. I was empty and cold. She had become someone it was hard to recognize; all my memories were of a big, rounded woman. In shape now she must look as she had as a young girl, small and slender.

'She never woke up,' my father said. 'Her breathing got rough and stopped. She just drifted away.'

'It was for the best, Dan,' Biddy murmured. 'She'd only have suffered otherwise. Will we pray for her soul?'

They knelt by the bed, my father lowering himself with difficulty. He took his beads from his pocket and started the *Misericordia*, a prayer that they'd always said at the end of the rosary, part of the often lengthy 'trimmings' that my mother liked to attach;

'Hail holy Queen, Mother of Mercy, hail our life, our sweet-ness and our hope; to thee do we cry, poor banished children of Eve, to thee do we send up our sighs, mourning and weep-ing in this vale of tears . . .'

Their voices joined, Biddy's higher tones skimming his low rumble. I held the bedpost, watching their bowed heads and my mother's wasted face. All I could think of were the lines from that song. They went around in my head; I could hear her singing them, putting little flourishes on some of the notes:

> And I'd kiss him far into the night-time
> With kisses worth silver and gold.

ELEVEN

I hadn't realized how quickly everything moved in Ireland once a person died. I was used to daily events meandering along; I felt cloaked in my English persona most strongly whenever I tried to force a date for something to happen. The bottled gas for my parents' cooker would always be delivered 'sometime next week'; the turf-man merely mentioned the month he'd turn up. My mother died on Monday and I was startled to discover that the funeral would be on Wednesday. My father decided to keep her at home until the Wednesday morning, when she'd be taken to the church. He'd stick to the old ways, he said, and hold the wake with her there; he wasn't going to have her stranded in a lonely funeral parlour.

Dermot seemed philosophical about her dying just before he arrived. He swung into the practicalities of the death certificate and funeral arrangements. I took my father aside before he set off in Dermot's car to see the priest about the service.

'Did you know Mum bought a shroud? She showed me it. She wanted to be buried in it.'

He was buttoning up his coat. 'One of those awful yokes she saw in the paper?'

'That's right.'

'I knew she would, I knew she was up to something. I said it was a gloomy-looking object, she'd be better in one of her frocks, but that was your mother all over. '

'I'll give it to Biddy, she's going to help the undertaker.'

He nodded. 'Where had she hidden it?'

'Bottom of the wardrobe. It's not that bad; brown, simple, a bit monastic.' God, I thought, I sound like a fashion commentator.

'Her mother had one, I suppose that's why she wanted it.' He leaned against the wall for a moment.

'Are you okay? Are you sure you're up to going with Dermot?'

'Yes, yes. It'll do me good. She's not to be left, now.'

'No, there'll always be someone with her.'

'That's tradition,' he said, 'that's an important one. She wouldn't want to be left lonely, she always hated that. I won't be long.'

It was late afternoon, the time of day in winter that she found most melancholy, when shadows lengthen and a hush descends. Biddy was sitting with her, waiting for the undertaker to arrive. I got the shroud out and showed it to her. She nodded.

'I didn't know you could still get them. They were very popular at one time.'

'Apparently Nana wore one; I never saw her in her coffin.'

'Oh yes, she'd had one for years.'

'You weren't at her funeral.'

'No.' She sighed. 'We'd quarrelled. I don't know if you were ever told, but before I left Cork I had a son who went for adoption. She wanted to raise him herself but I said no. I couldn't face the idea that he'd be here, I knew I'd never be able to make a clean break. We wrote for a while, but she was forever reminding me about him in her letters and once I'd met Roy I was worried he'd read one and ask questions.'

'Roy didn't know?'

A ghost of a smile passed over Biddy's face. 'Not until many years after we were married. It was different then, Rory; women kept things like that to themselves in case it put men off, even men who wanted to marry them. "Damaged goods" was a phrase you'd hear. It was part of the reason I kept away from

Kitty, too. I never knew if she might mention it in front of Roy.'

I remembered her saying in the car that Roy hadn't wanted to visit Ireland. Now I wondered if it had been more a case of her wanting to keep him away.

'Did you see your son before he was taken for adoption?'

'I had him beside me for one morning. I called him Brendan to myself, but of course that wouldn't have been his real name.'

I replaced the low-burning candle next to my mother, wondering if Biddy kept herself so carefully because if she allowed a crack to form, grief would pour through. One son cold in the ground, another out there somewhere, lost to her as effectively as if he were dead.

'Mum always put a lighted candle in the window on Christmas Eve,' I said. 'It was to guide the lonely traveller and to invite Christ in.'

'Our mother used to do the same. You'd see it flickering as you came up the glen. I always loved the sight of it; it guided you to the place where you belonged.'

'I don't know much about what happens now, Biddy. Will the coffin be in here?'

'It can be put wherever we say. I think in here would be best; it can rest on the bed.'

She unfolded the shroud and laid it out ready at the foot of the bed.

'I saw my mother prepare a dead person once, a woman who was a neighbour. She was so gentle, she talked away to her as she was doing it. I'll have a chat with Kitty as I wash her.'

'I'll sit for a bit now,' I told her. 'You get a cup of tea.'

She straightened her jumper. She must touch up her face regularly during the day, I thought; her make-up always looked flawless. At the door she stopped, stroking her palm down one of the badly-painted panels.

'He'd be fifty next February, Brendan,' she said.

I sat looking into the candle flame. My mother's body was before me, but I was thinking of another woman, a woman

168

who so hated the thought of her grandchildren being adopted, she had saved one and tried to rescue another. Then a thought came into my mind; what if she'd done the same with Brendan as she'd managed with Ita, waiting until Biddy had left on the boat and then going to the nuns? He might be out there, not far away at all, thinking that his mother was dead. Or she might have cooked up some other scheme for him, invented another set of relationships completely. The only person who might know was lying silent before me. I couldn't say anything to Biddy because I'd promised not to reveal the other story about Ita. What would Biddy gain from it even if I could? It was pure surmise on my part; fifteen years separated Nellie and Biddy and Nana might have been well past the stage when she wanted to bother with another infant by the time Brendan was born. For many years I had found my mother's family bewildering in its silences and feuds; a kind of irritation used to come over me when I contemplated their arguments, pregnancies, conspiracies and disappearances. Now I saw how easy it was to be drawn into the webs they had spun, how once one started to weave its way round you it was hard to escape; you were pulled inexorably into its depths. I would leave well alone, stay silent, knowing that my silence added another strand to the tangled skein.

That evening, for the first time since I'd arrived, I didn't know what to do with myself. Biddy and the undertaker were preparing my mother, Dermot had made calls to inform people about her death and was taking a long bath, and my father was marking prayers he wanted read at the funeral in a mass book. The house felt full and busy, but I was restless. I had been for a walk in the sharp night, but the darkness seemed hostile and I stumbled. The thought of her drew me back, making me turn and hurry; it wouldn't be long now before she was in the frosty ground and I would have only the pictures in my memory.

'Is there anything I can be getting on with?' I asked my father.

He lowered his glasses and chewed the end of his pen. 'We'll need grub for the wake tomorrow night, you could make a list. Will you take Biddy to buy stuff in the morning?'

'Of course. How many will be coming?'

'There'll be ourselves, Una and Con and some of their boys, and God knows how many others. You'd better get enough for the five thousand.'

I started on a list, but I couldn't concentrate. I kept expecting her to call for us or ring the stuck-up lady or to hear the rattle of her blackthorn stick. A couple of the Christmas cards we'd written were still waiting to be delivered. Her tube of ointment was on the mantelpiece; I thought of how when she'd been rubbing it in she used to fail to remove it completely from her fingers so that you'd be picking up traces of it when you touched things after her. It wasn't unusual to take a cup of tea she'd poured and find a liniment flavour on the rim.

When the undertaker had gone we all went in to see her. The coffin had been positioned across the bed with her head to the fire and feet to the door. Candles burned at the bed's four corners. She looked weary but tranquil in her brown robe, her hands with the rosary on her breast. Her hair had been neatly brushed back and tucked behind her ears. She'd have approved, I thought, saying so to Biddy.

'You've done a grand job,' my father nodded. He was going to go to bed early, he said, and keep her company, but before that maybe we could all kneel and say a decade of the rosary?

I had no idea if Dermot practised his faith or not. He had come from the bathroom with eyes stung by more than shampoo. Now he reached into his trouser pocket and pulled out a rosary. My father glanced at me and without further thought I knelt, assuming a position that was at once foreign and completely familiar. My father led us off. I murmured along with them, recalling all the words with no difficulty, clasping my hands loosely in front of me. I'm doing this for you, I said silently to her, but it's a one-off; if you're watching you needn't think it's going to become a habit.

While my father went to the bathroom I placed a clump of rosemary I'd picked in the coffin, pressing it down beside her. Then I took one of the cologne wipes from its sealed packet and smoothed it across her brow and on her chin. My little ritual completed, I whispered goodnight to her and left her to her sleep and her last nights with her husband.

The following day was a hasty blur. Biddy and I loaded shopping trolleys in Fermoy; cold meats, cheeses, bread, spuds for baking, soft drinks, fruit juices, wines, spirits. I asked Biddy what drink she liked, knowing that she'd say a cream sherry; a moderate little tipple with a touch of refinement. At the check-out she blew out a breath.

'It's ages since I bought so much at once. D'you think we've got enough ham and stuff?'

We'd discovered that we were both vegetarians. Neither of us could gauge how much the carnivores might work through.

'I think so,' I said, reckoning that nobody's bone marrow was going to be under threat.

We got back to find Dermot wearing one of my mother's cross-over aprons and wielding lavender polish. The house was spick and span, the cleanest I'd ever seen it.

'Where's Dad?' I asked.

'In with Mum. He gave me a clear run at the place. Any idea why she had bags full of silver foil stacked by the fridge?'

'Probably saving it up for some appeal or other.' I was thinking that she might have been contemplating a new hobby and had been building materials; foil collages, maybe.

I opened their bedroom door and glanced in. My father was nodding in the chair, one hand resting on the foot of the coffin. The room felt quite different to the rest of the house, a quiet place apart.

At six, Una and Con arrived with three of their sons, closely followed by Mr and Mrs Kelly and four other neighbours. My father took them in formally to see my mother, then they migrated to the kitchen for food and drinks. The house quickly filled up while I was unloading baked potatoes from the oven, and I heard fleeting phrases of the comfort being offered to my father:

'. . . sure she was a grand woman . . .'

'. . . Isn't it as well she didn't suffer long . . .'

'. . . Ye'd made a great go of this place . . .'

'. . . Any time at all, drop in and see us . . .'

'. . . Didn't she make a lovely garden out there where it used to be all nettles . . .'

I skimmed faces that had become slightly familiar in the last fortnight and others I'd never seen, observing the texture of the life my parents had been living here, one that I had touched intermittently but barely knew. I had that feeling of apprehension that children experience when they first realize that their mother and father are individuals who had whole years of life before they became parents. I touched a warm potato to centre myself in the here and now. A pair of thick glasses sitting on a pudgy nose appeared in front of me and I stared, recognition dawning.

'Is it Denny?' I asked, my heart lifting.

The face was shoved in towards me for a close look.

'Yerrra, 'tis me all rrright. And ye'd be Rrrorrry, wouldn't ye?'

I shook his hand, realizing that I was having no trouble understanding him. 'That's right. I used to come on your bus.'

'Wisha, dat's yearrrs ago now.'

'It is. I remember it well, though, going off to Cork. It was always breaking down.'

'Dat ould ting! 'Twas a wrrreck, surrre.'

'Can I get you something?'

He glanced at the drinks. 'I don't suppose ye've any Little Norrra limonade?'

'I don't think so.' I picked up a bottle of white fizzy stuff, nothing like the still, light-orange drink he'd loved. 'Would this do?'

'Ah, I suppose. I tink dey've stopped de Little Norrra now. I miss it terrrible.'

I watched him pile a plate with food and make a face as he sipped his fizzy drink. He was stooped now and his hair had vanished. I peered around the table at his feet; he was wearing highly-polished black shoes with his dark suit. Did he still take off to Athlone I wondered, and if not, what type of sanctuary had he replaced it with?

The bedroom door was propped open so that my mother could hear the talk and the singing that started up as the evening progressed. A crowd gathered around the fire. Dermot gave us a song about Ned Kelly, Biddy sang 'She Moved Through the Fair' and we had choruses of all those familiar ballads I'd learned instead of 'Humpty Dumpty' and 'Jack and Jill'. Biddy was sitting beside me, flushed with the heat of the fire and several sherries. I turned to her.

'Can I ask you something?'

'Go on.'

'What exactly happened with the trifles?'

'Ah, God.' She ran a finger along her bottom lip, a thing I'd often seen my mother do. 'Kitty sprinkled hundreds and thousands on top of them. They looked awful. I said something – I can't even remember what now – and she went berserk.'

'She was a bit mad for those hundreds and thousands at one time,' I said, 'they appeared on everything.' I could see them now, coating the tops of puddings and biscuits like rainbow-coloured insects. It was always like that with food; something would take her fancy – glacé cherries, candied fruits, marshmallow shapes – and it would be added to every dessert. Sometimes it was a kitchen implement that dictated the fashion; when she bought a potato scoop we were served rounded balls of mashed potato for weeks until we begged for a change. The worst trap to fall into was to acknowledge that you had liked a particular dish, macaroni cheese with chopped tomatoes, for example. Then it would be presented to you for evenings afterwards until the very sight of it made you nauseous; when you feebly suggested that it might be time to ring the changes, she would put her hands on her hips and say that she was driven demented with the food fads that went on around her.

Biddy shook her head. 'It's ridiculous when you think of it; what a thing to fall out over.'

Knowing my mother, it seemed entirely in keeping; in fact, I found the explanation deeply satisfying.

I sat for a while, listening to the songs and picking out Denny's fine tenor voice. The rumble of conversation and the selection of old tunes, with differences of opinion about their provenance and the airs they could be matched with created a comforting backdrop. I felt as if life had been put on hold, caught in this warm hollow by the glowing turf.

Near midnight, Dermot went out to freshen the teapot and I followed him after a few minutes to round up the rest of the snacks and bring them to the fire. He was standing with the kettle in one hand and a cup raised to his nose.

'What on earth . . . ?' he said, taking a sip and proffering the cup to me.

I sniffed at the dark-brown liquid. 'What are you trying to make?'

'Coffee. Look.'

He showed me a jar which did indeed bear a label stating 'coffee'. I took it, nipped one of the dark-brown granules out between my fingers and put it on my tongue. I chuckled.

'It's gravy,' I told him. 'She moved things around containers; don't ask me why. Those are gravy granules.'

He stared at me. 'She could be a complete and utter fruit basket.'

I nodded, smiling.

'So where would the coffee be?'

'Haven't a clue, I never drink dried stuff. The flour bin?'

He muttered, opening cupboard doors. I pulled back the curtain and looked out of the window. The taste of meat stock was on my tongue; you got me, I acknowledged, you managed to slide a morsel of animal down me at your wake. I pictured the cocky smile she'd give when she'd got her way, folding her arms across her chest.

Dermot's shadow was on the glass, moving impatiently along the shelves behind me, examining containers. I turned to give him a hand.

TWELVE

I went to bed in the early hours after the wake ended, wondering if I would dream about my mother, but the only thing that disturbed my sleep was Denny's stertorous breathing. It turned out that he had hitched his way to us from Bantry with just the clothes he stood up in. He assumed, with a genial expectation, that things would fall into place, that there would be somewhere to rest his head so that he could attend the funeral. Raking around at two in the morning, I found an old blow-up mattress that had been in the back of the cupboard for years; it might well have been the one that he'd slept on the time he had surfaced in Tottenham. Dermot and I took turns inflating it by mouth and we laid it on the floor in the little room where we were sleeping.

Denny took off his shoes and suit and climbed into his sleeping-bag wearing his shirt, tie and underclothes. He zipped himself up with satisfaction.

'I've neverrr shlept in one of dese yokes beforrre,' he told me, ''tis like putting a leterrr in an envelope.'

Dermot opened the window a notch. 'I think we'll need a bit of oxygen overnight with three of us in here. You must have been to a good few wakes in your time, Denny. Did we do all right?'

Denny lay back, his bald head like a smooth egg on his pillow. ''Twas a good sending-off and de singing was shtrong. But wakes in generrral arrren't what dey ushed to be. We ushed to wake de dead forrr two whole daysh and nightsh and de whole of de parish would be dere. The tay dat was dhrrrunk and de rosharrries dat werrre said! Still, dem ould daysh is gone and dat's all dere is to it.'

A moment later he was asleep, his tie hanging outside the sleeping-bag.

I lay for a while, reflecting on those vanished days he'd referred to. Less than a century ago, my mother's death would have been an occasion that absorbed the neighbourhood for the best part of a week. Afterwards, my father would have been left with his family around him and a close-knit community where people thought nothing of dropping in to each other's houses in casual companionship. His sorrow and his children's sorrow would have been shared and assuaged. By the end of this week, my father would be alone in a silent house, all the bustle stilled; Dermot would be back in Hong Kong, Biddy in Southend, myself in London. His neighbours, distanced from each other by cars and jobs, would keep an eye on him, but there would be no regular visiting. Here he would be with his thoughts and the hundreds of reminders of the woman he'd shared his life with. Lines of a poem translated from the Irish came to me:

> I parted from my life last night,
> A woman's body sunk in clay:
> The tender bosom that I loved
> Wrapped in a sheet they took away.
> The heavy blossom that had lit
> The ancient boughs is tossed and blown;
> Here was the burden of delight
> That long had weighed the old tree down.
> My body's self deserts me now,
> The half of me that was her own,
> Since all I knew of brightness died
> Half of me lingers, half is gone.
> The face that was like hawthorn bloom

Was my right foot and my right side;
And my right hand and my right eye
Were no more mine than hers who died.

I drifted into sleep, thinking that I would ask him if he wanted
to come back to London with me for a couple of weeks at least,
but knowing he'd refuse. I doubted that I'd even get him
to budge for Christmas; he liked his own bed, he'd say, his
grumbling bones couldn't adjust to foreign ones these days.

The undertaker arrived at half-past eight the next morning
to take my mother to the church. My father followed the coffin
out to the hearse and when it had been installed, he patted
the rear window as if in confirmation that he'd see her again
soon. The morning was mild and sunny.

'She'd say we chose a good day for it,' I said as my father
came back in.

'She would indeed. Is Denny awake?'

'In the bathroom.'

'And is all the transport worked out?' He fiddled edgily with
the top button of his shirt.

'Don't worry, Dad, we've got it all sorted.'

'I want this to go as smooth as clockwork.'

'It will. Wasn't Denny amazing, getting here under his own
steam?'

My father nodded. 'Your mother always used to say that
God keeps a special eye on the simple-minded.'

As we drove to the small parish church at mid-morning the
sun was high and clear. Biddy and Denny came in my car, and
my father travelled with Dermot in his. Biddy had only a vague
recollection of Denny from when she was a child, but they'd
got into conversation at the wake and were talking ten to the
dozen on the short journey to the funeral mass. Denny was
reminding her of great aunts and uncles; a Michael who'd
been in the British Army in India, come back to Bandon with
a handsome pension and been shot by the IRA during the
civil war. His body was never found, said Denny, even though

my grandmother had gone to the local brigade chief and begged to be told its whereabouts. Then there was a Tessie, a real good-looker, who'd emigrated to America and was said to have played a bit part in a Gary Cooper film.

I listened, thinking that I must visit Denny sometime and learn what I could about relatives I'd never heard of. It seemed that my grandmother had often been looking for people, dead and alive. In 1940, I recalled, she'd spent a week in Cork trying to pick up a trace of the missing Jack. My mother had described her coming home exhausted and in tears, mourning her eldest son.

As I turned at the crossroads leading to the church a sudden thought struck me; what if Ita appeared at the mass and came back to the house afterwards? I didn't see how she could possibly know that my mother had died, but word got around fast on the rural grapevine; Denny might have mentioned it to someone who knew the postman who came to Ita's cottage. I would have to explain how I knew her, and she might ask questions of my father or Biddy which would unravel ancient history and give Biddy a terrible shock. She'd said to my father that my mother was the last of her sisters; this was no time to discover that there was yet another twist in the family's knotted story.

I scanned the church carefully as we walked in. It was nearly full, but I couldn't see any sign of Ita. I thought back to John-Jo staggering towards my grandmother's grave, and had a vision of a shower cap appearing in the cemetery as we interred my mother. I focused, picking up a hymn sheet, realizing that I wouldn't be able to relax completely until we were back at the house.

My mother's coffin rested just below the altar. There are only three times when we can be sure of being the centre of attention, my father had remarked on the eve of my wedding; at birth, marriage and death.

Father Brady came from the vestry and the congregation stood. He bowed to the coffin, blessed it with incense and ascended to the altar. How many years was it since I'd been at mass? Twenty-five, I reckoned, not counting the end of one I'd caught one Christmas Eve when I'd arrived to pick up my parents from the midnight service. I had no idea how things were ordered these days; when to kneel, rise, sit, make a response. I felt like an actor who hasn't learned his lines or moves properly. I studied the pamphlet provided and saw that instructions were given at certain points.

Father Brady gave a three-minute, general sermon about life and death; the trials here, the bliss before us if we had faith. He finished by saying he was sure that my mother, a good and generous woman, was enjoying eternal happiness. I found it bland, but she would like it with its simple assurances. My father had chosen hymns she favoured; 'Lead Kindly Light', 'The Lord's My Shepherd', 'Hail! Bright Star of Ocean' and a modern ditty I didn't recognize, a toe-curling happy-clappy song that I stared at the floor through. Then came a prayer I recalled well, one that I had learned in Latin during my own devout period, Psalm 129 for the dead. It had been read at the funeral of Mary Quinlan all those years ago in Twickenham and its dramatic verse had grabbed my attention. I whispered it in Latin as Father Brady intoned it: 'De profundis clamavi ad te, Domine; Domine, exaudi vocem meam.'

> Out of the depths have I cried unto thee,
> O Lord; Lord, hear my voice.
> O let thine ears be attentive to the voice
> Of my supplication.

We came to the lines that I found particularly moving, ones that I was sure my mother, with her love of the dramatic, would approve:

> My soul hath waited on his word:
> My soul hath hoped in the Lord.
> From the morning watch even until night:
> Let Israel hope in the Lord.

Tears came to my eyes then. I fervently hoped that she had reached the place she had yearned for.

There were no surprises at the cemetery, just a noon sun, a quiet final blessing of the coffin and handfuls of earth thrown gently down. My father stood on his own by the grave for a moment, his rosary hanging in his fingers; then he leaned down and added the rosary to the flowers and earth that were already blanketing her.

I drove back to the cottage with Biddy first; we'd said that we would see to the last-minute arrangements for the food that she and Dermot had prepared after breakfast. A small group of people were expected.

'What do we veggies have instead of funeral baked meats?' I asked her.

'How about funeral roast nuts?'

I told her about bone marrow going missing and she laughed.

'Oh, Rory, I do wish all those years hadn't gone by without a word.'

I nodded. 'That's just the way things are sometimes.' The mass, with its echoes of my religious education, had triggered memories for me; myself sitting with my mother, reading through the Devotions for Confession in my missal before my confirmation. Father Corcoran would be coming into school to ask us questions and check that we were properly prepared. My mother was going to make sure that I shone in these studies. There were exercises for the conscience, to use before confession:

> Have you offended anyone by injurious, threatening words or actions? Or spread any report, true or false, that exposed your neighbour to contempt, or made him undervalued? Have you been forward or peevish towards anyone in your carriage, speech or conversation?

My mother had sat with a pious expression listening to me parrot the words while I pictured her and Assumpta bickering

181

by the lockers. I wondered what she confessed in the wooden cubicle at the back of the church; she never seemed to be in there for long and her penance took only a few minutes, which didn't suggest any major sins to be forgiven. Maybe she didn't identify herself in those conscience exercises or maybe, with her inclination to bargain, she weighed things up and felt that she compensated for those faults by adhering to principles in the other exercises; behaviour in relation to God, for example:

> Have you spent your time, especially on Sundays and holy days, not in sluggishly lying in bed or in any sort of idle entertainment, but in reading, praying, or other pious exercises; and taken care that those under your charge have done the like and not wanted time for prayer or to prepare for the sacraments?

She had certainly worked hard at ensuring that I fulfilled my religious duties. If I was part of the trade-off for her failings it must have been a deep shock, much deeper than I'd realized, when I renounced the faith.

I poked and stacked up the fire in the living-room. Biddy laid a lace cloth on the table and set out sandwiches and pickles on the plates I'd washed – the china set with rosebuds that my mother had kept for very best. I gave her silver sugar-bowl a buffing and filled it with sugar lumps, setting the delicate tongs on the top. The huge yellow and green cheese dish she'd bought in Muswell Hill, with the handle in the shape of a stocky ploughman, sat centre table; the ploughman held a hand over his eyes, forever peering into the distance.

'Kitty had some lovely things,' said Biddy, admiring the silver tongs, 'real quality.'

'She was always saying she should go on one of those antique programmes, to have stuff valued.'

'Oh, she had an eye, certainly.'

We were a more muted gathering than at the wake, but by no means sombre. The priest came and sat with my father for a while, accepting a cup of tea but no food. He was on a diet, he explained to me ruefully, patting his tum. My father winked at me and said there wasn't much we couldn't tell him about diets. Dermot had taken a box from the cupboard and was going through old photos, showing them to Biddy and Denny. He looked in an envelope and handed a small white book to me.

'Here, holy Joe, this has got your name in; from the time when you were one of the fold.'

It was my old missal. She'd kept it safe; just in case I became unlapsed, presumably. My childish hand was on the inside cover and various holy pictures free-floated amongst the pages. Flicking through it, I saw that I was a member of societies I'd completely forgotten: The Apostleship of Prayer (all members get a plenary indulgence on admission and on the first Saturday of each month), The Union of the Little Flower (a spiritual union to spread the Kingdom of God by prayer) and The Convocation of the Holy Trinity (the members will be included in Vatican masses in the spirit of reparation). Examining the certificates for each of these, I noticed that the last two were dated 1986 and 1993; she had signed me up without my knowing.

I slipped out of the back door into the garden. It was nearly three o'clock and the sun was dropping. Her favourite cat, a malevolent-looking mustard and white female, shot past me into the hedge. The ratty dog up at the farm barked four short barks. The ground would be getting cold now, I thought, and she nestling in her shroud, unaware. I crouched and pressed my palm on the damp rosemary, crushing its springy leaves so that its aroma reached up to me.